BAD
BOY

Also by Dream Jordan

HOT GIRL

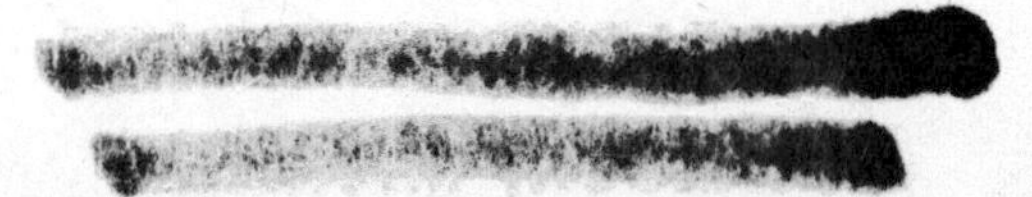

Dream Jordan

Bad Boy

St. Martin's Griffin
New York

This is a work of fiction. All of the characters, organizations, and events portrayed in this novel are either products of the author's imagination or are used fictitiously.

 Printed in the United States of America. For information, address St. Martin's Press, 175 Fifth Avenue, New York, N.Y. 10010.

www.stmartins.com

ISBN 978-0-312-54997-8 (pbk.)

ISBN 978-1-4299-2689-8 (e-book)

10 9 8 7 6 5 4 3

To all Survivors

Acknowledgments

I'm now two books strong and still blessed in my Dream Team: Daniel Lazar, my sharp and dazzling agent, Sara Goodman, my amazing and extremely perceptive editor, Kia Dupree, an early believer in my work, who has put her editing pencil aside to pen her own novels, and the entire St. Martin's Press staff, who helped bring my book to life.

Many, many thanks to all who gave me invaluable insight and feedback for my work. Big shout-out to those of you who consider yourselves true-blue *Hot Girl* fans. Your encouraging messages are invaluable. You make me blush.

And what would I do without all of the wonderful librarians and teachers who have spread the word about Kate? A toast to you! I'm so happy to have met some of you, too. Special thanks to PEN American Center; it is always a pleasure and an honor to work with your organization.

Finally, I am deeply indebted to all of the special people in my life who have supported me in times of doubt, and cheered me up just by being there throughout my writing journey. You know who you are.

BAD
BOY

Prologue

This time it wasn't my fault.

On the last day of June, I was leaving the Johnson household and headed to my thirteenth placement. This day I had dreaded for so long. Standing by the front door, baggage by my side, I faced my foster parents, playing my best tough-girl role. "Y'all don't have to wait outside with me," I said.

"Are you sure?" asked Lynn, her light-skinned face red from crying.

"Yeah, I'm good," I lied.

Lynn reached out and hugged me so tight I almost lost my breath. Ted hugged me, too, then hastily let go. I could tell he wanted to cry just as bad as me. His hair was so much grayer than I remembered. Usually jolly as can be, he now looked plain old miserable.

I quickly looked away from Ted. No need to prolong this sad scene. I had rehearsed an unemotional departure in my mind for an entire week. Just needed to say my good-byes and be done with it. "Well, guess I better go," I finally said.

Wearing a fake smile, I flashed them the peace sign, swung open the front door, and stepped outside into the late-afternoon air. As soon as I closed the door, my smile instantly faded, and my heart sank inside my chest like a torpedoed battleship. I felt so defeated, so alone.

As I struggled down the porch steps with my enormous red suitcase on wheels and two black duffel bags hanging from each shoulder, a rusty blue van pulled up to the curb. "Hello there, young lady," the baldheaded driver called out his window.

He received a polite nod instead of hello. I was in no mood for chitchat and he looked like the chitchatty type. He opened his door, about to hop out and help me with my bags. I stopped him cold flat with an outstretched hand. "No thanks," I said, "I got this."

I heaved my bags onto the backseat, climbed inside the van, fastened my seat belt, and stared dead ahead. Didn't dare look back at the Johnsons' house, just in case they had snuck outside to watch me go away. Listen, the sight of my foster parents standing on the stoop waving good-bye would only make my situation sadder, harder. Harder for me to build up my guts in order to face the drama sure to follow. Never thought I'd have to see the inside of a group home ever again. Well, never say never. The Old Kate was supposed to be dead; stomping out chicks in my distant past. But now, there was a good chance I'd have to bring her back to life.

"Nice day outside, isn't it?" asked the driver.

I put my mouth on mute.

"Weatherman threatened rain," he continued, "but look how sunny it is outside . . . that's why you can't believe everything you hear. Gotta go by what you see."

Seriously?

Hoping this dude would get a clue and be quiet, I turned my head away from him, and silently stared out of the window at the sun-drenched streets and people bustling about. "We're headed to the boondocks," the driver said with a chuckle. "Hope we don't get lost. Do you know your way around Brooklyn?"

I shrugged and continued staring out of the window. I wasn't trying to be rude to the guy, but I just couldn't muster up the strength to make fake conversation. Luckily, he finally took the hint and zipped his lips.

The driver smelled like a cheeseburger; I rolled the window all the way down. Warm summer air blew on my face, but I felt so cold and empty inside. The farther we got from Bed-Stuy, the emptier I felt.

As the van rumbled down Ocean Parkway, I took in my surroundings, bland as white bread with no butter. All I saw were tall trees and short houses and barely a soul hanging around town. When we turned off the parkway and headed down a side street, I realized we were getting closer to my dreadful destination. My eyes watered up against my will. Tears began to flow down my face. I furiously swiped at my eyes.

Keep it gangster, Kate.

We're almost there.

Oh, best believe, crying was not an option. Boohooing in front of my new housemates would only bring on their bullying faster. They'd take me for a silly punk and test me till I flunked. I should know. I wrote the script on this.

And as I stood in a huge shabby living room being given the stink-eye by five hard-looking chicks, I realized the script was now flipped. What goes around comes right back, and like a backhanded slap, I was *it*. Three girls were huddled on a sagging plum-colored couch. Two sat on the floor, eyeballing me nonstop. I felt like a juicy steak they couldn't wait to tear up. When Mrs. Cooper, the ancient group home supervisor, pushed me forward to introduce, nobody cracked a smile.

Mrs. Cooper patted my hand. "Kate, I promise you're really going to like it here."

Me, like it here? Please, picture that. My spirits plunged with the evening sun as I took in my surroundings: grim green paint covered the living room walls, cigarette-burned brown carpet covered the floor, and the smell of dirty feet and corn chips swirled up my nose. I'm saying, the Johnsons didn't live in a mansion, but at least they kept their home clean and funk free. This home, way out in Gravesend,

Brooklyn, was not the place to be. I was already plotting an escape in my head. . . . Straight up fantasy though, because I had no place to go. No family to speak of. No power to make my own moves. As a ward of the state, the system has me yoked up by the throat until I turn eighteen.

Mrs. Cooper smoothed down her gray crooked Afro with her bony, wrinkled hands and said, "Now for the rules."

I followed her out of the living room. She walked with her body bent low, slow as a turtle. Behind my back, I heard one of the girls say, "Dang, her cornbraids is mad fuzzy!" Wow, clowning me already, I thought.

Mrs. Cooper had either heard the diss and pretended not to, or she was plain old hard of hearing. Whatever the case, her frail little self probably couldn't discipline a fly.

"Yo, peep her dusty wardrobe," another girl piped in. Then they busted out laughing louder than necessary.

See? The dumbness was really going down. But I swallowed a nasty comeback and kept my dusty butt moving. Who cared that I was rocking a faded black T-shirt, and busted blue jean shorts? Worrying about my gear was so last year. No reason for me to pop off on these broads to gain respect. Been there, done that. Got me nowhere.

I had bigger and better things to worry about. Had to get on my grind before it's too late. In two more years, I had to be college-bound. Four years after that, I had to be on point—or be homeless. Basically, at age eighteen, you have the choice to stay in foster care or get out. But by age twenty-one, the only choice is to let the door hit you where the sun don't shine.

The system is dead serious like that. You could be living in foster care one minute, and in a cardboard box the next. My old roommate, Roberta, proved this simple fact. Last year I had bumped into her while she was begging on the number 3 train. The saddest sight I'd ever seen: Roberta was ashy and embarrassed, but trying hard to play it off. I tried to play it off, too; meanwhile a lump stayed stuck in my throat. I was staring at my own future if I didn't get it together. So, like I said, bump these silly broads. I had to stay focused on what really mattered.

Mrs. Cooper stopped short in front of a giant white poster hanging on the wall. Rules numbered one through ten were written in gigantic red letters. The rules that stuck out the most involved fifteen-minute phone calls, a crazy early ten o'clock curfew, and no boys calling the crib until you're sixteen years old. Well, I had a month and some change before I could think about a boy calling me.

Then again, I had no boyfriend to think of. Couldn't seem to meet any boys worth my time. All they did was holler at my big butt instead of trying to make love to my mind. Real talk, it was downright hopeless for me in the romance department. I'm saying, could a girl get some love, please? My last kiss had happened last year with a two-timing chump named Charles, who had taken my kindness for weakness, and played me for a fool. So if it wasn't love kicking my behind, it was foster care kicking me to my next location. I couldn't help but wonder if my life would ever change for the better.

"Any questions?" asked Mrs. Cooper, jolting me back to the present. She ran a long bony finger down each rule, to make sure I understood each and every one.

But all I wanted to ask was: "Why am I here? Why can't I *ever* live a normal freaking teenage life? Why was I ripped away from the first foster parents I could ever truly call Mom and Dad? It made no sense to me. I finally had a family to call my own, and then all of a sudden, I had to leave them? Just like that?

Everything had happened so fast. On a cloudy April afternoon we got the sad news: Ted's father was deathly sick in South Carolina. One month later, the Johnsons' roof literally fell apart. Next thing I know, the Johnsons are moving down South at the end of June.

The only upside of this: I found out Ted and Lynn actually wanted to adopt me; it was the first time in my life a family actually wanted to *keep* me.

Unfortunately, the Johnsons were so broke they couldn't afford to pay attention. With all of their backed-up bills and family complications, no amount of pleas or paperwork could convince the state that relocating down South would be a stable move for me. It was decided that I had been through enough disruption in my life already. Bottom line: I had to stay in New York without my family.

I remember the discussion about my future like it was yesterday. I was sitting on the living room couch flanked by Ted and Lynn, with attitude written all over my face. Tisha, my former (and best ever) social worker, was busy trying to convince me that this move was for the best. But all I could do was stare at the floor, my arms folded tightly across my chest.

"You have a ton of resources while in the system," Tisha explained, as worry lines creased her entire forehead. She could tell I was tight.

"Yeah, okay," I muttered. "Tons of resources."

"And staying in the system will help you get money for college—"

"Man, listen," I interrupted, "staying in the system is helping me go insane. . . . I'm tired of this moving-around mess."

"Trust me, I understand," said Tisha.

I knew she meant well, but her understanding didn't help my situation. I shook my head in disgust, feeling hopeless, helpless. "I swear I can't take this anymore," I said.

"What do you mean, you can't take this anymore?" Ted suddenly piped in. "You're a survivor, missy. This world can't stop *my* Kate!"

Ted and his silly self. He was only trying to make me feel better, even though it wasn't working. Lynn, the more serious one, simply said, "We're always going to be your family, Kate. Always remember that."

Comforting words at the time.

But right about now?

I was feeling mad uncomfortable, left to deal with group home staff instead of family. There would be no hugs here. No jokes. No love. Somehow, getting kicked out of people's homes was much easier than growing attached to them. I had only known the Johnsons for a year and a half, but it felt like I had known them my whole entire life . . . and now, *poof*, they were gone. Just like that.

"Kate, you seem so far away," said Mrs. Cooper, bringing me back to the present.

By now my tears were welling up again. But I quickly dammed up my eyes.

"Are you sure you have no questions for me, sweetheart?" she asked, staring at me with what looked like pity in her eyes.

I shook my head no, but wanted to scream, "Please, leave me alone already!" I had no freaking questions. Everything was crystal clear. Ready or not, I had to serve my time at the Common Grounds group home. Keep my head up. Control my temper. Make it out of this hellhole alive.

Chapter 1

I don't know what I was expecting, but I wasn't expecting *this*. As soon as Mrs. Cooper left me alone inside my bedroom, I wanted to call her old butt right back, and ask, "Are you serious right now?"

I looked around the shabby room in disbelief. Junky and funky—the first words that came to mind. In other group homes, we were never allowed to leave clothes sprawled on the floor, or food floating around in our rooms. Yet here I was, staring at a mountain of dirty jeans sitting in the middle of a stained gray carpet, and a half-eaten hot dog resting on top of a cheap wooden dresser. Four walls were covered in chipped beige paint, and white dirty blinds hung from the single window in our room. Twin beds sat across from each other. One bed was surprisingly decked in clean white sheets, the other was mad messy.

Earlier in the day, I was told Tracy was to be my roommate. Well, Tracy was a straight-up slob. I unpacked my bags with a serious attitude. Man, I missed my old bedroom so much. Although it was small as a shoebox, at least it was *mine*. Didn't have to share it with *nobody*. And I missed the Johnsons even more.

In the Johnson household, I had no big beef or worries. As soon as I had stopped acting like a knucklehead and learned how to return the love they gave me, it was so easy and breezy living with them.

Once my chores were done, it was all about creating my own program. I could chill by myself and watch the portable TV they'd bought me last Christmas (for getting all As on my report card), or I could sit up in bed and do homework in peace; I could play Spades with Ted, or have girl talks with Lynn; I could lounge on my fire escape, reading good books and cracking sunflower seeds. Real talk, I had it made in the shade while living there.

But here? *Please.* No peace up in this piece. Nobody to talk to. Nowhere to break away from the madness. Even the fire escape connected to our bedroom was located in a weed-filled backyard with a view of a corroded cemetery beyond it. How mournful could things get? I was ready to cry again.

After stashing all of my clothes away, I sat on my bed and leaned my head up against the wall, wondering what to do next. I wasn't trying to go downstairs and beg the girls for friendship. I could hear them from upstairs, talking and laughing loud, bonding nicely without me. Well, my room was disgusting; I needed to bond with a broom.

I jumped up and tried to make my bedroom more livable. Cracked open the window to let in some clean air. Using my foot, I pushed the pile of jeans closer to Tracy's side of the room. Then I kicked her sparkling white Adidas underneath her bed.

And just then.

Boom.

The second my foot connected with Tracy's sneakers, here she comes, sheathed in a tight sky-blue jean jumper and silver gladiator sandals, hands on her hips, scowl on her lips. I had the worst timing in the world.

Tracy is a shorty like me, dark-skinned like me, thick body like me, but she wears a long burgundy weave and has slits for eyes. She was using them to glare at me right now, trying hard to scare me. Not possible, though. I stood my ground.

"Yo, why are you kicking my things around?" Tracy snatched her sneakers out from under the bed and placed them in full view, to spite me, I guessed.

"My bad," I replied. "Sorry."

"Yeah, right, *your* bad," she snapped.

"I *said* I was sorry," I snapped back. Her attitude was so unnecessary. When someone apologizes to you and they really mean it, accept it and move on, silly chick. I had no time for this.

I looked at Tracy like she was minor league, and dared her to say something else. She had nothing more to add. So I marched right past her out of our bedroom, and braced myself for a possible attack from behind. But Tracy just called me the "B" word when I was halfway down the hall. I guessed she was all mouth, no action. Weak witch.

I decided to take a trip to the bathroom, for no other reason than to be alone. I pulled the rickety door closed with its flimsy (pray-nobody-busts-in) hook in the hole lock. Clicked on the light, which was mad bright, revealing all the grime surrounding me. Stray hairs and blue soap scum decorated the sink, a see-through plastic shower curtain revealed scummy tub tiles. No bath rugs in place. No pretty pictures on the wall. The main attraction: a noisy toilet with dirty brown water swirling around inside. Ugh. Straight-up nasty in here.

Thank goodness I didn't need to use the bathroom yet. I just needed to be alone for a few. I pushed the shower curtain aside and sat on the edge of the tub, feeling crazy depressed and out of it. Then someone pounded on the door, bringing me back into it.

I heaved a lungful of air, and stepped out of the bathroom to find Makeba, a pierced-up brown-skinned chick, doing the two-step like she had to go real bad. "It's about time," she huffed in a husky voice.

I flashed her the illest mean-grill and kept it moving. It felt like I had to be in defense mode 24/7. I'm saying, it felt like the whole house was against me for no apparent reason. I just couldn't understand it . . . but then again I could. I had played the same dirty game back when I was all about bullying. The new girl gets clowned on until she proves herself. *Yeah, I get it.* But now that the combat shoe was on my foot, it hurt like hell . . . drafted in a war I wasn't prepared for.

I couldn't complain to Mrs. Cooper about how the girls were treating me. No snitching is my rule—street code in my blood. And the other two grown-ups in the house, Belinda and Gerald, were a big fat joke. They could care less about encouraging us girls to get along. I could already tell they were just there to collect paychecks; chilling around the crib like a couple of stone-faced simpletons.

I had absolutely no one to confide in, to comfort me. I wanted to scream at the top of my lungs, "Get me out of this madhouse!" But if I screamed, who would hear me? Even my new social worker was *ghost*. She never returned my calls. I don't even remember her name.

I had nobody. Absolutely nobody.

When Mrs. Cooper called me down for dinner, I lied about a stomachache. Wasn't in the mood to be sitting at the table flanked by these skanks.

From upstairs, I heard their forks and knives clanging while my stomach was sangin', "Kate, what's going on? I'm starving like Marvin!"

Later that night, I tossed and flipped around in my strange new bed, hungry and restless. I couldn't sleep for nothing. Meanwhile, the whole house was catching zzz's. I had to do something to keep myself busy or I was about to lose my mind. I had left all my novels back in my old bedroom; had no magazines to flip through, no nothing to do.

Just then, I remembered my Lifebook, the book given to me by Lynn, the book Ted had told me to keep all of my experiences in. "Kate, you need to capture all of your life's moments," he had explained. "Big things, little things, good times and bad . . ."

Well, these times were bad and I needed to capture them. Then maybe one day I could look back and release them, saying to myself, "After all of the hardships you've experienced, look how far you've come."

Careful not to wake Tracy, I eased out of my bed and slid my knapsack from underneath it. I crept downstairs, hoping no one would block me. The hallway lights were on, but thank goodness not a soul in sight to stop me. I went into the living room, turned on the end table's lamp, and sank down on the couch. I pulled out my Lifebook, opened it up, and quickly flipped past all of the pictures of me and the Johnsons. Looking at those pictures would precipitate a rainstorm inside of me.

From my knapsack's side pocket, I pulled out my favorite fancy black felt-tip pen Ted had given me, and stared at the blank page staring back at me.

Now how should I begin?

My first day here and I hate this dirty stinking house. These chicks are asking me for problems, but I can't be snapping necks anymore. I have too much to lose. Too much I've already gained by changing my old ways. I know if Tisha were around, she'd tell me to suck it up and be strong. And I know I can be strong. Sometimes I forget that I'm a survivor. Always have been. Always will be. So let me stop tripping. I can do this. I can really do this. Nobody can bring me down, but me.

Seeing these words in print eased my mind. I repeated the last line out loud: *Nobody can bring me down, but me.* I wanted to believe in these words. I needed to believe in these words. I clicked off the light and sat up in the dark, repeating these words over and over again. I felt a little crazy, but what else could I do? I had no one around to put my mind at ease.

Finally, my eyelids got heavy. I made my way upstairs, feeling peaceful, maybe even a little hopeful about the rest of my stay at Common Grounds. From now on, I could write down all of my pain and frustrations, I reasoned. My Lifebook would be my lifeline to sanity. But three days later, bump a freaking journal. I was ready to choke a chick to death.

Chapter 2

The drama began brewing in the dining room.

I was sitting at the long wooden table, slumped over my plate, staring sadly at soggy scrambled eggs and cold sausage patties. I had gotten used to Lynn's slammin' feasts; I'm talking hot creamy cheese grits, juicy turkey bacon, and warm flaky biscuits with melted butter on top. And now *this*?

The girls were busy chomping away like this was the best meal they ever had. Meanwhile, all I could think about was how much weight I was going to lose while living here. Hungry as I was, I could only take one last bite out of my sorry sausage before finally giving up and pushing my plate forward.

"New Girl's turn to do the dishes," Makeba suddenly cried out as she jumped up from the table.

The other four girls looked my way, waiting for me to react. I shrugged, and said, "No problem." But I wasn't about to skyrocket out of my seat. I sat still for a minute, just to show them I had some spunk. Kate, a pushover? Please.

"You have to do them *now*," said Ciara, a tall, beady-eyed broad. "We don't let dishes sit in the sink."

It was too early in the morning for some bull. To avoid a scene, I got up, gathered the rest of the plates, and quietly walked into the kitchen. I gently placed the dishes in the sink, soaped them up, and scrubbed them sparkling clean. Before drying the last dish, a random little mouse poked his head out of the nearby stove's burner, as if to say, "Welcome home, Kate!" I wasn't scared of mice, so I didn't drop a plate; I just felt even more disgusted with my world. So this was my new life? Coping with bold rodents and silly broads? Wow, what a way to live.

From the kitchen, I had a clear view into the living room where the girls sat in front of the television, two on the floor, three on the couch. Then I glanced over at the far corner of the room where a large wooden bookcase filled with board games sat. I peeped a box of Checkers and Monopoly from where I stood.

A part of me wished I could bulldoze the barricade between me and these girls and just sit nice and pleasant with them playing games all day—I'm Queen of Monopoly, okay? But I knew I'd never get to reign here. The only game these chicks were interested in playing was: Let's Make Kate Miserable. There was nothing I could do to be cool with them; they clearly had it in for me, no matter what.

To test my theory, I lingered in the kitchen in full view of them. Just chilling. Idling about. Would someone be strong and throw Kate a bone? Ask me a question? Crack a stupid joke? *Something?* Even in my baddest days, I used to interrupt my bullying agenda to make the new girl feel included every once in a while.

So let's see. My kitchen location wasn't working. I inched closer to the living room, leaned against the archway, and looked at the TV from a safe distance.

Still no luck.

The group was busy talking mad loud during the commercial break, paying me absolutely no mind.

"Yeah, the Fourth of July gonna be off the hook in my hood," yelled Venus, a scrawny girl from the Bronx.

"You already know, *ho*," said Makeba, laughing.

"Y'all so stupid," cried out Asia, the flyest girl in the house. She reminded me of my foul-living, ex-friend Naleejah. Both chicks rock fake hazel eyes, silky long weaves, and slutty gear. "I'mma be flossin' in my boyfriend's BMW on the Fourth. Hair done, nails done, everything big!"

"You always bragging, B—" said Venus.

"Yeah, instead of bragging, come pick us up in the Beamer, trick!" cried out Makeba.

Asia laughed like it was a joke. They called each other disrespectful names all the time. Said mean things to each other for no reason. I quickly snapped out of wanting to be cool with them. I wanted to be out. Had to be out. Maybe not today. But at least for the Fourth of July. I hoped it wasn't too late to sign up for the volunteer opportunity I had already turned down.

A week ago, my best and only friend, Felicia, had asked me to volunteer with her for the Bed-Stuy Community Garden's annual July 4th celebration. A fund-raiser for the homeless. Now, I love a good cause, and you know I love The Stuy, so I told her I was in. But the next day, Felicia told me her man, Marlon, would be joining us. Oops, no offense; I'm out.

Not that I had a problem with Marlon. He was mad cool. But whenever I hung around the lovey-dovey couple, I stuck out like a sore loser. So rolling with them as the third wheel had been out of the question. But now? Considering my current chaos? I was ready to roll in third place, fourth place, whatever it took to get me out of *this* place.

I ran upstairs, found the volunteer coordinator's phone number in my backpack, and ran back downstairs to call the office. Our communal phone was located in the hallway, less than fifty feet away from the occupied living room, now under enemy control. No such thing as a private phone call, so I kept my voice low, trying not to call any attention to myself.

"Mr. King at your service!" the coordinator exclaimed. (Yes, this is how he really answered the phone. Mad extra.) And he sounded even jollier when I told him I wanted to volunteer. "Great to have you on board, Kate!" he shouted. Then he gave me a quick rundown of my duties.

"What time do you need me there?" I asked.

Before Mr. King could answer, I felt a tap on my shoulder. I spun around to face Makeba. "How long you gonna be?" she grumbled.

"I *just* got on the phone," I said in my calmest tone.

"Well, I need to use the phone *now*," she replied, clearly cookin' up some beef to boil. But I decided to let the silly chick stew for a minute.

"Be off in a second," I said.

Makeba huffed and sashayed away.

I got back down to business. "Mr. King, sorry for the interruption. What time do you need me there?"

"Ten o'clock sharp."

"No problem. See you then."

I hung up the phone softly so as not to get caught by the phone police. Then I picked it back up to call Felicia. We were allowed fifteen minutes for phone calls and my *full* fifteen minutes I would get.

"Hey, girl, can't talk long," I blurted, before Felicia could say hello. "So I'll see you at the Garden, and—"

"Oh no," Felicia interrupted.

"What do you mean 'oh no'?" I asked.

"I had to give up my position," she explained. "Marlon's performing poetry at the African Street Festival tomorrow. He's a last-minute addition to the show. I'm so excited. This is a big deal for him!"

"Um, okay," I said, feeling deflated, like a stabbed balloon. I was really looking forward to seeing Felicia. Blocked from my best friend. Again. Bad enough our whole school year had already put a wedge between us.

Basically, our new high school is populated with more kids like Felicia, barely anybody like me. Felicia's life is upper crust, while my life is crusty. So when Felicia made friends with this stuck-up duet, Brittany and Janette, I knew I wasn't going to be hanging with my homegirl too tough anymore. I couldn't stand these chicks. Black like me, but couldn't relate to my world. They talked in fake high-pitched voices, shopped exclusively on Fifth Avenue, and bragged about their countless trips around the globe—I'm talking Africa, France, Italy, Japan. Meanwhile, the most exotic place I've ever been to is Staten Island.

Funny, though—aside from world travel, I had no idea what Felicia saw in them. And it was mighty clear these girls were confused about me, too. I could tell by the way they turned up their noses, frowning and sniffing at me like they smelled a hood-rat.

Well, I'm far from a hood-rat. But I couldn't blame them for thinking that, since I got that Brooklyn swagger and I'm stuck with a C-shaped scar over my right eye. No doubt Felicia and I looked like a serious odd couple: nerdy girl and gangster chick prancing down our school's hallway.

But anyway.

I was seeing less of my homegirl because of Brittany and Janette. Now add Marlon to the mix, and you get a drifting friendship.

"Why do you sound so surprised about the festival?" asked Felicia. "I called the house yesterday to invite you."

"Wow," I exclaimed, shaking my head in disgust. "Nobody told me *jack*."

"OMG, you didn't get my message?" asked Felicia. "I called you around two o'clock."

"I swear, I can't stand these spiteful broads," I muttered. "I gotta get out of here, for real."

"See, that's why you need to hang with us," said Felicia. "I'll be helping Marlon's group all day, but you can lounge backstage with me while I work. You won't have to lift a finger, I promise."

"But I'll be the third wheel . . . as usual."

"You're not going to be the third wheel," she assured me. "There's going to be tons of people there. Lots of cute guys in Marlon's group, too. Don't you want to meet some cuties?"

"You know I'm not thirsty like that," I protested.

Meanwhile I was more than thirsty. Matter of fact, dehydrated. I wanted a boyfriend so bad I could drink him in my dreams. Seemed like everybody had a man, but me.

". . . . Come on, Kate. Please? I really miss you."

"Well . . . I already told Mr. King that I'd help him at the Garden. It wouldn't be right for both of us to diss him."

"But you can do the Garden *and* the festival," explained Felicia. "Marlon doesn't perform until five."

Hmm . . . rocking both events wasn't such a bad idea. The longer away from this madhouse, the better.

"Okay, I'll call you around—"

Suddenly, I heard Makeba's voice at the back of my head. "New Girl must think she running things 'round here," she rasped. Next thing I knew, the receiver was snatched from my grip, and the phone was hung up with a bang.

"Your time been up," Makeba snapped.

Oh. No. She. Didn't.

My bottom lip hit the floor. I stood frozen in my spot. Did that really just happen? I was in so much shock, I couldn't move a muscle.

Four years ago, in under sixty seconds, Makeba would've been drop-kicked flat on her back, with every silver piercing snatched from her stupid face. What? The Old Kate used to punch chicks dead in the mouth just for looking at her wrong. But this New Kate needed New Tactics.

So I locked my hands to my sides and mean-grilled Makeba for a minute. As angry as I was, I didn't say a word. This was such a proud (and painful) moment for me. Proud because I was so smooth with my 'tude, the other girls didn't even realize the craziness that had just gone down. Painful because I wanted to bash Makeba over the head with the phone, and I couldn't.

A split second later, the phone rang. I knew it was Felicia calling back to find out what just happened. Makeba snatched up the phone and said, "Check for her later. I gotta make a call."

Click.

I swear . . . if it wasn't for Tisha's voice in my head telling me to walk away, Makeba would've been calling 911.

So yeah, I walked away. Calm. Cool. Collected.

Before I had learned to walk away, I used to get into fights all day, every day. Some fights I would start, some I would not. It was all about maintaining my respect in any given situation. I thought I was the baddest chick in my school. Most kids agreed, and knew to steer clear of me. So imagine my surprise when Tisha called me a punk one day, straight to my face. I was sitting in the principal's office, fresh from a fight, my face all scratched up in zigzags. The principal had nothing to say to me; he needed Tisha to "reach" me.

"So I guess you think you did something," Tisha began. "Look at you!"

"Yeah, but I won the fight," I stated proudly. "These scratches don't hurt. I got the best of her."

"So where's your prize?" asked Tisha, cocking her head to the side. She wore a light brown curly weave that day, and it shook every time she moved her head. I wanted to laugh, but this was no laughing matter. Tisha was not playing with me. "Your face is all scratched up, and you're about to be suspended from school . . . so I'm asking you: Where's your prize for winning the fight?"

"But I bet that B— knows better than to call me out my name again."

"What did I tell you about cursing in front of me?"

"My bad," I said. And I only said, "my bad" to Tisha. No other grown-up had me in check like that. Tisha was the first social worker I had ever met who was *real*. From the hood and proud of it. The first day I met her she told me all about her wilding-out days and explained how she had to overcome a shipload of obstacles. I had much respect for Tisha because she wasn't schooling me from textbooks; she was speaking from real life. And even though she sat opposite me in her rigid navy blue suit, I knew that underneath her business front was a bad chick who could get down with her hands if she had to.

But at that moment, she was getting down with me—verbally—and her ferocity was astonishing. "Dang, calm down," I wanted to say. But I didn't dare.

"Kate, you let that girl play you," continued Tisha, her eyebrows knitted tight in anger. "And that makes you a *punk*. You hear me? A straight-up punk!"

I sat stock-still, staring at Tisha, blank-faced. The office was freezing cold from the air conditioner blowing on my back, and I just wanted to get the heck out of there.

"It takes a real woman to *walk away* from a fight," explained Tisha. "But you're always running *to* one. Are you going to throw up your hands every time somebody says something stupid to you?"

"I gotta do what I gotta do." I shrugged.

"And now you *gotta* get suspended. So like I said, Kate, you're a punk." Tisha pointed at me with her long fingernail to emphasize her point. "So go ahead and get left back in the sixth grade if you want to. You're the smartest girl in your class, yet you act so dumb! Always bragging that you never lost a fight, but there's always somebody out there bigger and badder than you. Remember that."

"Yeah, okay," I said.

"And if you ask me, I'd rather be a *living* punk, than a *dead* hero any day."

"But I *didn't* ask you," I wanted to say. Instead I just said, "Can I go now?"

"Not until you understand what I'm telling you."

"Yeah, I understand what you saying."

At the time, I was lying, I didn't understand jack. But during my weeklong suspension, I had a lot to think about. Tisha's words started ringing in my ears, oh so loud and true. And after reflecting on my countless battles with chicks over nonsense, I realized there were no trophies to show, no medals to wear. Where was my prize? What was my point? I had to face the fact: My life was a vicious cycle of violence for no good reason. It was high time for a change.

"Bawwwaaahhaa!"

The girls' loud guffaws brought me back to the reality that I was a "living punk" right now. Makeba had probably just told her telephone takeover story, and the girls were probably loving every detail of my humiliation. So despite my calming thoughts about Tisha's words, every step I took up the stairs caused my heart to skip three beats in my chest. Hearing their laughter rubbed salt into my wounded pride. I felt so disrespected, clowned on . . . forced to walk away? Oh man, I was tight. Nothing I could do but run upstairs, grab my Lifebook, and write.

I swear on my life, I better keep myself in check because Makeba is itching for me to snap her neck. She may be taller than me, but I've been known to knock down bigger broads flat on their backs. They used to call me "Rocky" for a reason.

And then there's Felicia. I'm happy Felicia wants to include me all the time. I know most girls would get a boyfriend and be like, Kate who? But homegirl needs to really fall back with this third-wheel crap. It's always pitiful, single me, hanging with a couple of lovebirds. Bird-watching just ain't my thing. I'm saying, when will I find a boyfriend to call my own? When will these spiteful group home chicks leave me the hell alone? I can't even lie. I'm feeling so hopeless these days. Every time I turn around, another smackdown comes my way.

Growing tired of my own pitiful words, I stopped my pen in its tracks. If I had continued writing like that, I was sure to start crying, and my Lifebook ain't waterproof.

I stashed my Lifebook in my duffel bag and covered it with a towel to conceal it. Then I sat on my bed and leaned my head against the wall and tried to think good thoughts. First thing that came to mind was the upcoming Fourth of July celebration. Not even a week spent at Common Grounds, and already I couldn't wait to return to my old hood. As sad as it would be, knowing Ted and Lynn were no longer there, I was still dying to return to Bed-Stuy. My present sucked so bad, a little touch of my past couldn't hurt . . . at least that's what I thought at the time.

Chapter 3

On Saturday morning, I jumped out of bed higher than a bunny on crack. I was so excited about getting out of the madhouse. But then I remembered my roommate, and calmed my happy self down. Tracy was knocked out cold with the sheets over her head, and I didn't want to wake her crazy butt up. She was not going to hold me back from hitting up my old hood.

I quietly rummaged through my drawers and pulled out a plain pink V-neck T-shirt, a pair of black baggy jean shorts, and laid the items out on my bed. My gear was corny as could be, but I didn't care; I was getting the freak outta here!

I took a cold shower—not by choice, there was no hot water in the joint—and raced back into my room, shivering cold. I silently got dressed. Finishing touches were my black dollar-store flip-flops, and then I dug up my beautiful silver bracelet from the bottom of my knapsack (carefully hidden from sticky-fingered bandits). Felicia had brought me this bracelet from South Africa and it meant a whole lot to me. The only genuine jewelry I ever rocked. Probably cost more than my entire outfit.

I went downstairs to find Gerald sprawled out on the living room couch, snoring like a pig, instead of watching us. I didn't know where Belinda was hiding. Mrs. Cooper was off for the holiday. So I was free to do me, no questions asked. The rules posted on the wall were mad bogus. This was the most lax group home I'd ever been in. Everything was done backward here; but since this meant my freedom could be achieved with so much ease, their careless sloppy system was just fine with me.

I went into the kitchen. Was about to hook me up a quick bowl of corn flakes. But then I peeped a mousetrap sitting on the stove. *Ugh.* Lost my dang appetite.

I signed myself out of the group home, hit the streets, and exhaled a big sigh of relief. I looked back at the shabby, three-story house wishing I could make it disappear with a magical stare. Two blinks later, nope, it was still there.

Our block was deader than a graveyard. Nothing but small brown houses, perfectly paved sidewalks, and Beamers and Benzes lined up against curbs. Not a soul in sight.

Come to think of it, I kinda liked things quiet and empty. At my other group homes, we had to deal with snoopy neighbors on the block peeping out of windows and doorways, giving us group home girls the side-eye every time we walked out the house. At least here, nobody was around to judge us, to mistrust us, to give us a hard time just for being in foster care.

Anyway.

The morning was cloudless and warm. I felt drama free as I breezed through the open air. The six-block walk to the F train was cool and uneventful. The train took less than five minutes to pull into the Avenue U station. It felt like it was going to be a very smooth day.

The feeling didn't last long.

My whole train ride to Bed-Stuy was jacked up. The "F" train must stand for Foul. First, there was a track fire, and then I was stuck in the tunnel for twenty minutes. Next thing you know, a passenger decided to get sick on the A train. Stalled again. I practically crawled out of the Utica Avenue train station, feeling hot, sticky, and beat.

But when I caught a whiff of the fresh morning air, I felt revived all over again. My emotions were running wild, up, down, and sideways.

The streets were alive in Bed-Stuy. Cars driving by pumping bass in the AM, people roaming around handling their business, firecrackers popping off in the far distance. Gravesend is a ghost town by comparison. Matter of fact, there is no comparison. I'll be reppin' Bed-Stuy till I die.

As I neared the front gate of the garden, tall trees with enormous leaves blocked my view of the inside. Then I stepped through the gate and was hit with a floral wonderland. Sunlight beamed from all different directions as I explored the breathtaking surroundings. Sunflowers and red roses were everywhere. A winding path made of red bricks led me to a cute little wishing well, then a pretty pond full of goldfish surrounded by big rocks, and then a towering willow tree with crazy shade underneath it.

The garden was huge, I marveled. Crazy space to lounge in. There were benches all over the place, and lots of cozy private corners to cuddle with your boo. . . . Too bad I didn't have one.

As I came across each nook, Felicia came to mind. She would have loved it here; and she was the main reason I even know what a "nook" is. Because of her, I could also name the "paper birch tree" situated in front of me, and the "sparrow" that just flew past my eyes. There was so much to learn while hanging with Felicia. So amazing how she went from being my seventh-grade math tutor, to my "life" tutor and best friend in the whole world. Too bad she wasn't here with me now. I really missed her.

A sudden rush of volunteers swirled around me from all sides. Some were carrying food to and fro, others were pulling weeds here and there. Out of the blue, a sweaty, short, stocky man who looked like Humpty Dumpty scurried up to me.

I was the only one not doing anything, and he wanted to change that. He had to be Mr. King. "Kate?" he asked, with his hand extended for a handshake.

He was so frenetic and fidgety I was tempted to deny it. "Yes, Kate," I finally admitted, shaking his clammy hand. *Ugh*.

"I'm Mr. King," he exclaimed. "Glad you're here! We need all the help we can get!" He waved his chubby arm forward. "Follow me."

I brushed past folks, trying to keep up with him. He led me to the back of the garden, and stopped short in front of a long wooden table.

"This will be easy work," he assured me, handing over a potato peeler.

Homeboy had me skinning a giant mountain of potatoes. Next thing you know, he had me shelling a mob of peas. By the time I was through peeling and shelling, I had rusty hands and green crap stuck underneath my stubby nails. I was hot, dumb hungry, tempted to eat some raw peas and potatoes. My day was starting off busted, for real. But when Mr. King gave me my next errand, I was ready to run for my life.

"I need you to pick up some donated paper plates and cups from the Fulton Street Market," he explained.

The Fulton Street Market?

Of all the stores in all the world, why did I have to go *there*?

"You know where the market is, right?" Mr. King asked.

I heard the question, but I didn't answer him. I was still stunned, like I had just gotten sucker-punched.

"Hello?" said Mr. King, twitching his nose like he had something up it.

"Oh, sorry, yes, I know where it is," I stuttered.

I knew the Fulton Street Market all too well. A few years ago, I used to terrorize the store's owner, Mrs. Thomas, with my old gang-banging crew, the Lady Killers. We were terrible with our madness.

I can't say she didn't deserve it, though. The first time I stepped inside her store she had disrespected me for no reason. "Miss, let me get a pack of sunflower seeds," I had said.

Mrs. Thomas stood behind the tall counter with her thick

eyebrows raised and she snapped, "My name is *Mrs.* Thomas, and it's not 'let me get,' it's 'may I have.' Your mother didn't train you better than that?"

Say what? Oh, your girl Kate was *hot.* This lady had some nerve talking down to me, as if speaking from a throne. She wasn't ruling anybody, especially not me. Time to put a chick in check. I stood on tippy toes, raised my pointer finger as close to her face as I could get, and said, "You don't know me like that, stupid B—"

Then I stormed out the store, making sure to slam the door. I usually don't call grown women the "B" word, but the lady had really gotten to me that day.

The next time I went inside the store was only because no other store had my favorite brand of fifty-cent chocolate chip cookies. I was five deep with my gangster girls this time, so I felt mighty powerful. We, the Lady Killers, wrecked worlds all day, okay? We had money in our pockets and we were ready to buy a grip of cookies and candy, and the oldest of my crew was going to hook us up with five forty ounces of beer. But before we could start picking up stuff, Mrs. Thomas sent her son Percy to follow us through the aisles, making sure we didn't steal anything. When we collectively peeped the dirty game she was playing, we were collectively pissed and wanted to do something about it. Icy set it off by saying, "Bump that, let's give her a reason to treat us grimy."

On the count of three, we spread out and ran through all four aisles, knocking down cans and bottles. Splashing and crashing everywhere. "Rocky, kick the glass in!" Icy yelled. My foot whapped at the glass enclosure in the front of the store, but it didn't break. "Yo, snatch some sour cream chips," yelled Killah. "I got you!" shouted Crash. Menace snatched up three packs of my favorite cookies and one forty-ounce beer, which was all she could carry.

Everything was happening so fast, we had Mrs. Thomas's and Percy's heads spinning. But Percy finally caught his bearings, and yanked me up from behind. Like a karate kid, I spun around and kneed him hard where it hurts. He let go of me, doubling over in pain. Then Icy kicked open the door and we all ran out, screaming and laughing like a wild pack of hyenas.

After that incident, you could find us in front of the Fulton Street Market giving Mrs. Thomas mad problems. Sometimes Percy would chase us away, sometimes Mrs. Thomas would call the cops. All the time, we had so much fun causing mayhem at their expense.

Funny though. Back then, I didn't realize how fine Percy was. In my tomboy days, dudes were the last thing on my mind. But about a month ago, I'd seen Percy outside, sweeping the sidewalk, and let me tell you, brother has it going *on*. From way across the street, I could see his body is *sick*, delicious muscles galore, towering tall, wrapped in beautifully smooth almond vanilla skin. His wife-beater tank top fit him oh so right. His swagger was out of this world. He had to be about eighteen or nineteen years old by now. Maybe a bit too old for me, but a girl can dream, can't she?

During my five-block walk to the market, a million thoughts ran through my mind. Would Percy remember me? Would Mrs. Thomas kick my behind for giving her such a hard time?

The only good thing was: I looked mad different. Back in the day, I used to rock my baseball cap pushed so low over my eyes you couldn't see my face, and my jeans were always extra baggy like a boy's. I was a thuggish ruggish broad back then. But now, at least I look like a female. My big boobies and booty are crazy hard to hide these days.

When I reached the front of the Fulton Street Market, I took a deep breath, and walked inside like an innocent little customer. The store still looked the same. Still smelled the same, like lemons. Bright overhead lights, shelves fully stocked, black-and-red tiled floor spotless because Percy was forever mopping.

Mrs. Thomas was standing behind the counter looking mean as ever. Her flawless brown skin wasted on a mean old face. She wore her usual green sack of a summer smock, and her thick eyebrows were knitted as if she had a 24/7 headache.

I approached her like a timid little kid.

She stared at me for a full minute, as if she had a moment of recognition. "May I help you?"

"Mr. King sent me for the cups and plates," I said in a soft sweet voice, hoping with all my heart she didn't recognize me.

"Percy!" she yelled. "Come out here!"

And that tall fine creamshake of a man emerged from the back room. He swaggered toward the counter, staring at me hard, just like his momma.

Did *he* remember me? I really hoped not.

"Bring me the bag for Mr. King," ordered Mrs. Thomas.

"Where is it, Ma?" he asked, in a deep voice.

"Do you ever *listen* when I talk to you?" asked Mrs. Thomas with her hands on wide hips. "The bag is sitting plain as day by my chair."

Percy rushed into the backroom and came back carrying a giant black plastic bag. He handed me the bag. "Here you go . . . *Rocky*," A slow grin crept over his lips.

My bottom lip hit the floor.

Percy jutted his chin toward me and said, "Ma, you know who she is, right?"

Part of me wanted to flee. The stronger part of me stood my ground. But my knees were made of liquid.

Mrs. Thomas frowned at me for what felt like an hour, and finally said, "Oh yeah . . . I *do* remember you. . . . You used to raise a ruckus in my store."

I lowered my head in shame. If I were light-skinned, I would've been beet red in the face.

She cocked her head to the side and added, "But I guess you've changed . . . hopefully."

I raised my eyes to meet Mrs. Thomas's. She was still staring at me with a deadpan look. Percy was standing next to her, a gleam of amusement pasted on his handsome face.

Mrs. Thomas broke the ice by saying, "Doesn't the party start at twelve? I'm sure Mr. King is waiting for you, young lady."

"Oh, yeah, thanks," I stuttered. "Okay, good-bye." I headed for the door, carrying the giant black bag with both hands.

Percy dashed ahead of me, and blocked the door with his beautiful body, spreading his arms wide. "I'm not letting you get away from me this time," he said, grinning.

"Quit playing around, fool," Mrs. Thomas yelled. "Let the girl go."

Percy flashed me a boyish smile, stared at me for long minute with his light brown eyes, and then held the door wide open for me to make my exit.

"Thank you," I said, without looking at him, still embarrassed as ever.

"My pleasure," said Percy, playfully bowing from the waist. "Come again."

Joking or serious, *heck no*, I wasn't coming again. I had made it out the store in one piece, and I wasn't trying to press my luck.

On the other hand, the fact that Percy said "come again" made me feel like he actually *wanted* to see me again. Really?

I mean . . . putting me on blast in front of his mother was not nice at all . . . but Percy's gorgeousness was so powerfully blinding that all I could do was sweat him in my mind.

Percy was so unique. Usually, super fine guys like him are too busy being fine—not playful. The way Percy had teased me as if he *liked* me or something was so unexpected and appreciated. I loved the way his smile lit up his whole entire face. I never had a guy stare straight into my eyes the way Percy did. Charles came close, but Percy's gaze was mad *intense*.

Point-blank, Percy had revived the girly feelings inside of me. I wanted to see him again. *Had* to see him again. But how? I don't believe in acting thirsty when it comes to boys. So I wasn't about to stalk his store.

What to do? What to do? How could I make my move?

I walked back to the garden with my new crush on my mind. But as it turned out, I had no time to plot on how to make him mine. To my surprise, I had another bombshell waiting for me around the corner: An old flame ready to light up Percy's spot.

Chapter 4

Charles.

My almost-boo, posted up by the garden's front gate, talking on his celly, looking too freaking good for words. I'm saying, why the fine men all up in my mix today? Before Charles noticed me, I took in all of his loveliness. His dark brown skin sweeter than chocolate, his towering six-foot frame posed like a beautiful work of art. He was dipped in his favorite royal-blue jersey and baggy khaki shorts hanging off his sexy behind, not enough to show his drawers, but just enough to show his swagger. No more waves in his hair. Now he rocked a blown-out Afro. I must say, my boy be mighty fly from head to toe.

But every time I see Charles, I try to look straight through him like he's a dirty window. Ignore the fact that he's a dime, and concentrate on the grime. Just when I was ready to give my whole heart to him, he played me for a chump. So why should I make the same mistake twice?

Yet and still, sad to say, Charles can make my stomach flip to this day.

"What's up," I said, as I walked up to him, trying hard to look nonchalant.

Charles looked in my direction and his face broke out into a giant grin, showing off dazzling white teeth, and a large wad of purple bubble gum sticking out between them. He told whomever goodbye and shoved his phone into his back pocket. "Kate, what's really good?" he exclaimed, reaching out to hug me.

I put the plastic bag on the ground and opened my arms wide. He held me for a long minute. His body felt so hot, a deep burning current ran through me. Oh man, I was getting flashbacks of the good old days.

Kate, remember the grime.

I caught my breath, pulled myself away, and said, "So what you been up to?"

"Same old," he replied. "I haven't seen you since what . . . May?"

"Yeah, that's about right." From the beginning of May till the end of June, I had stayed mostly in the house, mad depressed over my upcoming removal from the Johnson household.

"I missed you, Kate," Charles said. "*I really* missed you." He stared at me long and hard.

Whoa now. I didn't want to be catching feelings again. No need for us to go back *there*. Charles already had his chance, and he blew it.

I quickly changed the subject. "So, are you here to support the cause, like the good dude that you are?" I was being sarcastic by stressing the word "good."

"No doubt," he replied. "What about you?"

"I'm volunteering."

"Wow, that's really sweet of you," said Charles. "So where's your partner in crime?"

"Up Marlon's butt," I wanted to say. Instead, I just shrugged.

"Did Felicia tell you I've been asking about you?" Charles asked. "She gave you my number?"

"Yeah."

"Then why didn't you check for me? Too busy for me?"

"Nah, I'm just trying to do something with my life."

Charles smiled. "See, that's why I admire you. You make me want to do something with my life, too . . . we'd be so good together."

"Yeah, okay."

Charles closed his eyes and busted into song. "Baby you're my everything, you're all I ever wanted, we could do it real big—"

"Anyway," I interrupted, "the party doesn't start till twelve. Craving to get in, huh?"

"Craving for you," said Charles, lowering his eyelids seductively.

"Boy, stop playing."

"Playing is for boys," said Charles. "I'm a grown man now."

"Please, you ain't even old enough to drive yet," I teased.

"Seriously, I've *grown* a whole lot."

"You're still the same height if you ask me." Yes, all six luscious feet of him still the same. I loved craning my neck to look up at Charles. So dang fine, mm, what a shame.

"Seriously, Kate, trust me . . . I slowed down a whole lot. . . . It's real out there . . . I mean . . . well . . . you heard about Naleejah, right?"

"No, what happened?" I asked, crazy curious. "What did the hussy do *this* time?"

"I can't talk about that right now," said Charles, looking down at the ground. "It's not a good time. I just assumed you already heard by now."

I hit Charles in the arm. "Man, don't leave me hanging like that!"

"I'll tell you eventually . . . just not now."

"Aw see, you suck!"

"Anyway, I'm early because I needed to get out the house. Our air conditioner broke. I was sweating mad bullets in the crib."

"That's not a good look," I said, careful not to bring up my own home-life situation. No need to be sharing my pitiful business all the time.

Charles rubbed his sexy stomach. "Man, my mom's been bugging me to get this food all morning. She heard the spare ribs go quick. I gotta be the first in line. Feel me?"

"Yeah, I feel you," I said.

Mm, I wanted to feel *him*. Charles's arms wrapped around me again. Oh man, I was so confused about my outlook on him.

Suddenly, Mr. King spotted me through the gate, and frantically waved for me to come inside. I asked if Charles could come, too.

"Only if he's here to help," Mr. King replied hastily. I looked over at Charles. He shrugged and said, "I'll help, if it means I get to hang with you."

With every sweet line Charles laid, he was making it so hard for me to act aloof toward him. Luckily, the beautiful image of Percy kept popping into my brain. Percy's stunner smile and bangin' body was like whoa. It was time for a change anyway. Charles already had his chance.

But when Charles was ordered to pick up stray trash around the garden, and he said he was doing it "just for me," my heart skipped three beats. I watched his swaggerlicious moves around the garden, picking up trash just for me. Why were his legs so freaking sexy? Why did the sweat dripping down his face drive me crazy? I was in seventh heaven watching my boy work it just for me.

Then Mr. King busted my bubble by calling Charles inside a shed to break down boxes. From the look on Charles's face, I could tell he was pissed. I kinda felt bad for dragging him into this.

Ten minutes passed. Now Mr. King had me sitting at another small round table folding garden literature into pamphlets.

Charles suddenly came up from behind and whispered in my ear, "Yo, I swear this dude about to catch a beat down. Tell me why he's ordering me around like he crazy?" I flinched from feeling his delicious warm raspberry bubblegum breath in my ear. OMG.

Recovering my sanity, I said, "Well, help me with these, please?" I pointed to the heap of paper I had to fold. To tell you the truth, I didn't need his help; I just wanted his company a bit longer.

"Nah," said Charles. "Mr. Crazy already told me we can't work together. He thinks we won't get anything done. So I'm out. I'll be back for my food, okay, baby?"

See, why did Charles have to call me "baby" all out of the blue? You know how it gets when it's been a long time since you been somebody's baby. You lose your freaking mind. You conveniently forget the bad times and let the same doggish dude back in your life. My mind was such a murky mess right now.

To clear my head, and to take a break from pamphlet duty, I walked Charles toward the exit. Charles stopped short in front of the pond, dug a quarter out of his pocket, and threw it in before I could stop him.

"That's not a wishing well!" I said, grabbing his arm. "Don't you see the goldfish swimming around?"

"Oh, my bad," said Charles. He quickly bent down, fished his quarter out the water, and wiped his hands dry on his shorts.

"What were you wishing for . . . to choke the fish out?" I joked.

"Nah," Charles said. "I was wishing for your forgiveness . . . your one-hundred-percent forgiveness."

Oh boy. Now where did that come from? It was fine when Charles was joking about "us," but now I could tell he was dead serious. . . . Apparently, he knew I was still hurt. Must have been a case of classic Kate: I think I'm hiding my true feelings, acting like everything's all good, but somehow my innermost feelings always manage to shine through.

"Kate . . . it's not the same between us. I can *feel* it."

"Look, let's drop that already, please? What's done is done. We're good. Okay?"

"I don't believe you."

"Well, you don't have to believe me," I snapped, suddenly thinking how funny it is that dudes who do the dirt always try to act so freaking clean. They be on some *whodunit*, when *they* done it. Shoot, Charles needed to learn the word "accountability," just like I had to.

After beating up so many girls with no apology, Tisha had to drill it in my head that I was wrong; that I needed to accept responsibility for my own actions. Nobody *made* me stomp those girls out; so I fully deserved the trouble I was constantly getting into.

"You know what, Charles," I began, "you really need to stop acting so clueless. It's really annoying."

Charles stood in one spot, staring at me with sad eyes. "But you been on my mind for a long time. . . . I just wish you'd give me another chance."

Growing frustrated, I didn't want to prolong this pointless scene, so I finally said, "Anyway, like I said, we're cool. We'll always be cool. So can we move on, for real this time?"

"Yeah, okay," said Charles, staring at the ground. "We can move on."

"And listen, thanks for helping me out," I said.

"Anything for you, Kate . . . but you already know."

I flashed a smile, and quickly looked away before I got trapped by his hypnotic dark-brown eyes. My crush since the second grade had already crushed me once before. Never again.

"Mr. King is coming our way," Charles blurted. "Catch you later." He left the garden, gliding with that smooth walk of his that no one else can duplicate. I swear, his swagger was so official. Too bad his faithfulness was not.

Chapter 5

When Charles returned to the garden, a mob of people were already standing on a long line, anxious to get their grub on. Old-people's soul music was playing. The sun was shining brightly. It was turning out to be a really nice day. Surprisingly, Mr. King let the volunteers eat first, so I was already fed and relaxing in a chair near the front entrance when Charles walked up to me. "Hey, why didn't you save me a spot on line?" he asked.

"Shoot, why didn't you save *me*?" I countered. "Mr. King was riding my bra strap all day!"

"Well, I hope the food is as good as everybody is claiming," said Charles. "That line is way too long for it not to be."

"The food is mad good," I said, rubbing my belly. "Especially the potato salad. Trust."

"Mm, can't wait," said Charles, licking his sexy lips.

I was glad Charles seemed to get over his "forgiveness" question. I wasn't in the mood for rehashing old wounds. At the moment, all I could see were sunbeams spreading throughout the garden, all I could smell were burgers, chicken, and ribs simmering on the grill, and all I could hear was soul music pumping out of a nearby speaker.

"Kate, let's get this party started right," Charles said, grabbing my hand and hauling me out of my chair.

A corny old-school jam song was now playing, and the next thing I knew, we were dancing to it. Charles pulled me close to him, spun me around a few times, and I couldn't stop laughing as he sang off tune, jacking up the words to the song.

A trio of women stopped what they were doing to watch us. I heard one of them say, "Aww, they're so adorable. I remember when I was that age."

I must admit, we *were* adorable, and it was so rare for Charles to show his silly side in front of other people. He had a lot of hard-core friends holding him back from playfulness, just like I did . . . before I met Felicia.

When the song was over, I was out of breath from being whirled around. Charles was busy grinning at me like a schoolboy.

We sat on a long green bench located in the cut. Plenty of space on the bench, but Charles chose to sit so close our legs made delicious contact. Then he touched my hair out of nowhere. "I like your braids."

I laughed at this. "Picture that. These raggedy braids are almost two weeks old!"

"Doesn't matter, I still like them," he said, touching my hair again. My braids reached the middle of my neck. The warmth from Charles's fingers brushing against my neck had me going bananas inside.

"Shoot, I wish I had your hair," I said. "Yours is so much longer than mine."

"And you're so much prettier than me," Charles replied, reaching out to pinch my cheeks.

"Boy, stop!" I said, playfully slapping his hand away.

"I can't help it if I love your chubby cheeks." Then Charles started playing with my braids again. "So who did your hair?" he asked.

"Me," I said proudly. I had mastered doing my own hair two months ago. Before being shipped off to Common Grounds, Lynn had taught me how to be self-sufficient and braid my own hair. Now I could rock cute cornrows without paying a soul. Considering the pitiful allowance the group home gave, this was a really good look.

"So can you hook me up?" asked Charles.

"Of course I can."

"How much you charging?"

"You don't have to pay me, silly."

"Wow," said Charles, shaking his head. "See what I mean about you?"

"What?" I asked.

"You're so sweet."

"Oh, stop," I said, but I wanted him to keep going. I love hearing good things about myself. "So when do you want your hair done?"

"Today?" asked Charles, smoothing down his lovely mane.

It didn't take me long to think about it. The fund-raiser was over at five. I could be in and out of the African Festival before six. I was in no rush to go home. Why should I rush home? I could already picture Charles sitting on the floor in front of me, his luscious arms resting on my lonely little legs.

"Today is good," I said. "Around six o'clock, no later than seven?"

"Cool," replied Charles. "Call me when you're about to come through."

"Okay, let me get your digits."

"How you gonna lose my number, Kate?"

"My bad," I said. "I'm unorganized." But between me and you, I didn't *lose* his number. When Felicia had passed me Charles's new number, I threw it straight in the trash. Hey, I didn't want to be tempted.

But now, don't ask me how, I was kinda open to Charles again, as my make-believe boyfriend: someone I could stare at for hours, drool over secretly, and get my rocks off from a simple touch, or a hug; hey, he was better than nothing. At least I knew not to take the boy seriously anymore. You can never be disappointed when you already know what's up. Basically, I just planned to keep Charles far away from my heart and enjoy him up close and personal.

Charles grabbed a pen from the table, jotted down his cell number on a pamphlet, and pushed it my way.

I threw the pamphlet in my pocket and said, "It shouldn't take me too long to get at you."

"I'll wait for you forever, girl," Charles replied, with a wink.

He joined the long line to get his food, came back fifteen minutes later with two paper plates wrapped in foil, and before walking out the gate, he blew an air kiss at me.

I playfully blew a kiss back, thinking how much I missed "us." I missed us back in the day, how we used to talk for hours sitting on random stoops; I missed us buggin' out on the basketball court shooting hoops, playing defense—my favorite part—when his sweet chocolate body constantly bumped against mine.

Although Charles and I would probably never work out as a couple, he made me feel so good inside—even as my friend. And who knew. . . . Maybe we would end up like Tisha and her new husband, Greg. They were friends since grade school, too. Had their ups and downs. Greg acting like a clown, Tisha constantly turning him down. It took them over twenty years to figure out they were meant for each other. First, a reconnection on Facebook. Now they're married and headed to Paris in August. Such a beautiful love story . . . .

The only sad part: Tisha was on leave and no longer my social worker. She said I could call her anytime, but why would I? This was the happiest time in her life, and the saddest time in mine. If I called Tisha, I knew all of my new group home problems would be spilled, no matter how hard I tried to keep them stuffed inside.

"Kate, I need you to help me finish breaking down boxes," said Mr. King, jolting me out of my thoughts. "Your little boyfriend just abandoned me."

Boyfriend. I wished . . . well, sometimes, I wished.

I begrudgingly helped with the boxes. Then I sat back outside at the table with a heavy plop. With Charles gone, I suddenly started feeling lonely. I looked all around me. Everybody eating, dancing, and merrily chitchatting with each other. Me? By myself. Stuck at the table and bored to death.

Didn't last for long, though. Here comes Mr. King again, forcing a bunch of pamphlets into my hands, nudging me outside the front gate. As crowded as it was, he still wanted more people inside. He was raising money for the homeless and he wanted the world to know it.

I stood out front, doing my thing. Passersby either snatched the pamphlets from me, ignored the pamphlets, or wanted to talk for hours about the pamphlets. Growing tired on my feet, I was relieved when I got down to my last pamphlet; I gladly gave it away and called it a day.

I went back inside the garden and found an empty chair near the front gate. My feet thanked me. Ahhh, what a freaking load off! I hoped Mr. King wouldn't spot me for a while. I needed some time to rest.

A few peaceful minutes passed. I closed my eyes. Then opened them. Instinctively, I glanced toward the front gate.

Then *boom*.

I was hit with my third shock of the day.

Percy. In the flesh. Headed my way. His electrical smile aimed dead at me.

Chapter 6

My head was spinning from the sudden pull of two dudes. Percy? Charles? All in one day? Well, let me pop my collar, 'cause I didn't know I had it like *that.* I mean, Charles, I could understand. We had so much history. But Percy? I'm sorry. It just didn't seem possible that I could snag a super fine guy like him. No disrespect to me . . . I'm only keeping it real.

"Hey," Percy said, before grabbing a nearby chair.

"Hey," I replied, quite baffled.

"I'm on my lunch break so I can't stay long," Percy explained. "Just wanted to stop by and say sorry about earlier. . . . I shouldn't have put you on the spot like that."

"Oh . . . it's okay," I stuttered.

"Soon as you left, my mother jumped on my case like she always does. I didn't mean to make you feel uncomfortable."

"It's nothing," I said. "I did what I did back then . . . I can't deny that."

"Yeah, you were a wild child, for real!"

"It's embarrassing."

"But you shouldn't be embarrassed," said Percy. "Look at you now, volunteering . . . doing your thing."

I flashed an awkward smile.

"So what's your *real* name?"

"Kate."

"Pretty name."

"Thanks." I beamed.

Percy stared at me deeply with his clear light-brown eyes before saying, "This is my first time seeing you so up-close. Your skin is flawless. You look like a perfect ebony doll."

I looked down at the grass, blushing. Although Percy's words seemed like they were lifted straight from a romance novel, I was reading into it big-time, and loving every minute of it. The fact that Percy could appreciate my dark skin tone really made me feel good. I'm saying, turn on any commercial, movie, or music video, and you're never going to see a thick, dark-skinned girl like me being considered the object of beauty. Point-blank. Period.

Percy touched my hand. "So how can I make it up to you?"

I looked up into Percy's eyes, so beautiful and intense, burning straight through me. "Make what up?" I asked, in a daze.

"For putting you on blast," he explained, taking his hand away. "I feel really bad about that."

I was still so taken aback by Percy's magical appearance, I just didn't know what to say.

Percy tapped my leg, breaking me out of my trance. "Well, what are you doing later?"

"Oh, um, meeting my friend at the African Street Festival."

"Can I come with you?"

What? Could he come? My face lit up like a thousand suns. Of course he could come! Imagine me showing up at the festival with a hottie like Percy on my arm. No more pitiful third-wheeling. I'd be rolling with a serious dime by my side.

"If you want to," I said, hoping Percy couldn't hear the excitement bubbling in my stomach like gas.

"Cool," Percy began. "Let me get your math so we can coordinate."

"Oh, um, I don't have a cell phone."

Percy frowned. "Okay, I'll pick you up around four. Can you wait for me right here?"

"Yeah, I can wait," I said in my calmest tone. But oh man, I couldn't wait. I was too excited for words. The day couldn't move quickly enough. I wished I had a time machine so I could press fast-forward. Things were finally looking up for me, and it was about dang time.

Chapter 7

When two o'clock rolled around, I was ready to strangle Mr. King. He was on my last nerve, asking me to do every freaking thing when he had other volunteers chilling like villains in front of his silly-looking face. I could no longer take him in my ear, yelling, "Kate, do this! Kate, do that!" True, I'm young. But I ain't dumb. I don't let *nobody* take advantage of me. And if it wasn't for Percy's promise to come get me at four o'clock, I would've *been* told Mr. King to buzz off. Volunteering is one thing. Slavery is another.

So when I spotted Mr. King scurrying toward me carrying a large empty trash bag, I said to myself, nope, not trying to be his garbage girl. I ducked him by pretending I had to use the bathroom. After that, I dipped and dodged the terrible tyrant until a quarter to four. When Mr. King zipped one way, I zipped the other. Maybe I was wrong for deserting my duty; maybe he was wrong for treating me like a greasy slave. Whatever the case, I was too busy thinking about my date with Percy to really care at this point.

I still couldn't believe I had a guy like Percy checking for me. Shoot, I wondered if he would even show up. But my fears were laid to rest when Percy appeared by the front gate at four o'clock on the dot. I hurried up to the gate and slipped out real slick before Mr. King could ask me for another freaking thing.

"Hey," said Percy.

"Hey," I said, slightly out of breath.

"You ready?"

"For sure." I grinned to myself. I couldn't wait for Felicia to feast her eyes on Percy.

"I'm parked across the street," said Percy, gently touching my back.

We walked halfway down the block, when suddenly a loud cherry bomb blew up. My whole body jerked in surprise. Percy laughed and put his arm around my shoulder. "Don't worry, I got you."

With his arm still around my shoulder, he led me to a sparkling fire-engine red Dodge Avenger sitting on twenty-two-inch dubs. Windows tinted silver, so you couldn't see inside. I climbed into the car, feeling like a grown woman. I was riding shotgun, like what?

Percy gunned the engine, then he pumped some booming beats and we sped down the block in stunner style. I wanted to roll down my window to show off, but Percy had the air conditioner blasting, so I couldn't. I wanted to sit back and enjoy the ride, but Percy was speeding like a madman, so I couldn't. Thank goodness we made it to the festival in one piece.

From outside of the tall silver gates, I could see red-and-white striped tents and swarms of people spread out all over a huge field.

"What you wanna do first?" asked Percy, grabbing my hand.

Since it was close to five o'clock, I pointed to the large stage across the field. As we snaked in and out of people I spotted Marlon and Felicia standing on the sidelines, hugged up as usual.

Felicia was so easy to spot with her tall, brown, slim self. She wore a short green and gold African-print tank dress, and gold-studded flip-flops. Her shoulder-length hair was pushed back into the usual ponytail. Marlon, also tall, brown, but not so slim, wore an African-print green and gold short set, his hair in a simple fade. They must've planned to look like twins. How cute of them.

"My friends are over there," I told Percy, trying to hide the excitement in my voice. "Felicia!" I yelled.

Felicia caught sight of me, broke out into a grin, and came running toward us. She took one look at me, then at Percy, and I could tell she was mad curious. Meanwhile, all I could think was: Finally, a foursome!

"You made it," Felicia exclaimed.

"Hey, Kate, thanks for coming," said Marlon, grinning wide, showing the gap between his front teeth. They both looked over at Percy, expecting me to make introductions. Oops, I forgot. I'm new at this, okay?

Percy introduced himself, and then gave Marlon the homeboy handshake.

"So, is the show starting soon?" I asked.

"They're having technical problems right now," said Marlon. "We just have to wait a bit."

So we stood around small talking. Percy's beautiful smile was on flash the whole time. He was so friendly, and I was impressed. I hoped Felicia was impressed, too.

But then our conversation started running out. The sun was relentlessly shining down on us. We all started complaining about the heat, and the technical difficulties. We didn't want to "stand by" much longer.

Finally, Marlon and Felicia were summoned by an announcer on-stage. Felicia turned to me in mock exasperation. "OMG, all of this hard work for my boo!"

"But he's worth it," I said, with a chuckle.

Felicia smiled. Then she snuck a glance at Percy, opened her eyes wide, and raised her eyebrows at me. This was her secret signal that she couldn't wait to get the full scoop on Percy. Shoot, I couldn't wait to tell her!

"Okay, girlie, be back in a minute," Felicia called over her back.

After Felicia and Marlon were out of sight, Percy turned to me and said, "Your friends are nice."

"True," I replied, but suddenly thought I should've said "thanks" instead. Your friends are a reflection of you. So he was actually giving me a compliment, too.

Ten minutes passed. Finally, three men in orange African costumes carried drums and chairs onstage to set things off. Then, *boom*, the trio started pounding the skin out of those drums. A group of small kids in similar orange African prints came running out doing flips and tricks all across the stage. The drummers were going hard. I turned to Percy, smiling. He was standing with his arms folded across his sexy chest, nodding his head to the beat. He saw me looking up at him, so he bent down to my ear and said, "This is really cool. I'm glad I came."

I looked up at him and smiled.

When the drumming died down, Marlon strutted onstage, carrying a huge wooden cane. He planted it on the stage and started spittin' poetry, contrasting Africa and the streets. "From glocks and hard knocks, I rise above it. Respect my homeland, Africa, I love it . . ." His flow was tight. I was surprised he could even spit like this, living in the ritzy part of Park Slope, and having absolutely no swagger. . . . But he treated my homegirl like gold and that's all that really mattered.

After Marlon's performance, we gathered back together again.

"My dude, you did really good," said Percy, patting Marlon on the back.

"That was *fire*," I joined in.

"See, Kate," Felicia exclaimed, "I'm so glad you finally got to see Marlon do his thing!" She squeezed my arm.

"No doubt," I said. "So what's next?"

"Three more performances," said Felicia.

"But do you still have to help backstage?" I asked.

"Yep, after this break, I have to go back."

"Oh, okay," I said, not hiding my dissatisfaction. Shoot, instead of her helping backstage, she needed to be hearing the backstory on Percy.

"But trust me, the next performances will be awesome," said Felicia. "Outstanding costumes, the works! And then later on, we can head to the after party in Clinton Hill." Felicia did a goofy dance, shaking her shoulders, trying to drop it like it's hot. We all busted out laughing at her. She could be mad silly at times. That's why I love her so much.

In the middle of us cracking up, Percy grabbed my hand, gave the tip of my fingers a quick squeeze, bent down to my ear, and whispered, "I'm sorry, but the sun is really getting to me . . . I don't feel up to standing in one spot to watch another show. I'd rather walk around."

I was disappointed, but not about to complain. Percy was the one who had brought me here, and I wanted things to jump off on the good foot. Our potential relationship was like a pair of fresh white sneakers—not to be stepped on.

"So, are you guys staying for the show?" asked Felicia, staring at me expectantly with her big brown eyes.

"Percy wants to walk around," I said.

"Oh . . . okay," said Felicia, looking disappointed.

Marlon was the first to hug me good-bye, followed by Felicia.

Percy waved good-bye to them.

Just as we were about to walk away, Felicia came running back up to me. "I forgot to tell you, my parents planned a last-minute trip to Martha's Vineyard. We're leaving tomorrow morning. I won't be back till Friday."

"Oh," I said, feeling even more let down. Now I'd have to wait a whole freaking week to express my excitement over Percy. I was really looking forward to hearing Felicia's thoughts on him, too. Oh well.

"But I'll call you first thing on Saturday," Felicia exclaimed. "I promise."

"Okay, cool," I said, hoping I'd be able to use the phone in peace that day.

After Felicia ran to catch up with Marlon, Percy turned to me. "You ready to see the sights?"

"For sure," I said, brightening up a bit.

He grabbed my hand and we walked straight into the crowd. The festival was alive and popping. People, people everywhere, selling colorful African jewelry, beautiful artwork, hot wings and hot dogs, candles and candies—everything you could imagine was in sight. I quickly got over my disappointment about not having a foursome. I was having so much fun with Percy, a romantic twosome. He held my hand firm the whole time, like he was claiming me to be his. I felt so proud to be with him. Shoot, I noticed a few girls openly drooling over him. I couldn't blame them. I was drooling, too.

Percy stopped short in front of a tent full of aromatic candles and bath products. "Want something from here?"

I looked around and shrugged. Stuff looked expensive.

"Pick anything you want," he said, noticing my hesitation.

Word? Just throw it in the bag?

I wasn't used to being treated to gifts. Most I ever got from a guy was a Twinkie. So what should I choose? Bringing candles into the group home would be a no-no. I could see crazy Tracy setting fire to my bed. And taking a bubble bath in our dingy tub would be impossible. I could hear Makeba knocking on the door every two seconds just to spite me. Finally, I chose a bottle of coconut lemongrass body lotion. Smelled fabulous!

"That's all you want?"

"Yes, thanks," I said, thinking it's better to be grateful than greedy.

Percy shrugged, bought the fifteen-dollar lotion, and handed me the small lavender gift bag it came in.

After another half hour of aimless walking, and not much talking, Percy said, "I just thought of something else we can do."

"Okay," I said, ready for the next chapter.

Percy locked hands with mine and led me to his car.

Chapter 8

The sun was still shining high in the sky when Percy cruised into a neighborhood called DUMBO. I had never heard of the place, so I felt like a dumbo. How could I be reppin' Brooklyn all day without knowing *all* its parts? I foolishly shared my ignorance with Percy.

"You never heard of *DUMBO?*" he repeated with raised eyebrows.

"No, I haven't."

"You don't get out much, do you?"

"No, not really," I replied with a shrug, trying to appear nonchalant instead of naïve.

"Well . . . we'll have to change all that." Percy smiled at me.

"So where are we going now?" I ventured to ask.

"You'll see," replied Percy mysteriously.

After a half hour of driving around, Percy finally pulled into a parking spot close to the Brooklyn Bridge's huge caissons. He walked around to let me out of the car like a perfect gentleman. Then he grabbed my hand like he was my man. Hmm, I could get used to this, I told myself, and then I wanted to pinch myself to make sure I wasn't dreaming.

As we walked over cobblestone streets, and passed rich houses and restaurants, Percy kept quiet. I wished he would talk to me some more. I wanted to know more about him without me having to give away all my business first. For instance, back in the car, Percy had asked me how old I am. I told him straight out. But when I asked him, he chuckled, and said, "Older than you." I didn't let the mystery of his age bother me that much though. We weren't in too deep . . . just yet.

As we passed by a pier, a wedding photo shoot was taking place. "Wow, she's so pretty," I blurted, at the sight of the beautiful bride decked in a flowing white lacy dress.

Percy finally opened his mouth again and said, "I can see you in that dress, one day. I know you'll make a gorgeous bride."

Awww.

In a flash, I pictured Percy as my handsome groom, Felicia as my maid of honor, Ted walking me down the aisle . . . okay, let me stop.

"You're a really pretty girl," said Percy, staring down at me. "You know that, right?"

"Thanks," I said, beaming.

Feeling giddy by Percy's words and this totally surreal day, I practically floated down the block. But when Percy halted in front of a tan six-story apartment building, I descended back down to the pavement.

"Hey, are you okay?" he asked.

"Yeah, I'm good," I lied. I didn't know where Percy was taking me, didn't know what he was expecting. If he thought he was getting sex *this* quick, he thought dead wrong. A girl has to take her time when it comes to the bump and grind. Rushing things be busting things, feel me?

I could only comfort myself with the fact that I knew Percy's mother. And Felicia knew who I was with right now. Percy couldn't be *that* bold to do anything crazy to me. Besides, up until now, he had been nothing but a gentleman.

I followed Percy inside the crystal-clean building, and we rode the elevator up to the sixth floor in silence. He pulled out a ring of keys and walked up to the first door on the right. "My dad's spot," he finally explained. "He's away for the summer."

We stepped inside the apartment and my bottom lip hit the floor. The place was baaaddd. Plush shaggy beige carpet covered the living room floor, a glass entertainment center sparkled like a jewel, a giant flat-screen television took up a whole living room wall, and floor-to-ceiling windows provided a dazzling view of the ocean. Like I said, the place was baaaddd.

Percy motioned for me to sit on the butter-soft beige leather couch, and he plopped down beside me. I was still looking around the room with my mouth wide open. All I could say was, "Wow, this is tight."

"Thanks," Percy replied. "When I need to get away from my mom, I come here . . . cool getaway, right?"

I nodded, in awe.

"See, if it was up to my mother, my dad wouldn't have all this. He does a lot of traveling as a business consultant, and he makes mad money doing it. My mom didn't want him out of her sight when they were married, so of course they got divorced. Now she's trying to pull the same mess with me. But I'm nineteen years old. A grown damn man. I go where I please, when I please."

Awkward.

This sudden outpouring of info was the most Percy had shared with me the whole day, and I didn't know how to respond. But at least I knew his age now. A bit too old for me. But then again, we weren't sexing or anything, just getting to know each other. No harm in that.

"My mother won't even give my dad his last name back," Percy continued, as if talking to himself. "She doesn't *deserve* his last name."

He looked so frustrated. Luckily, he soon changed the subject. "You hungry?"

I nodded.

"Okay, I'll order pizza . . . you like buffalo wings too?"

"My favorite," I said.

"Then I got you!" Percy laughed.

He jumped up from the couch, ordered our food, and then slid back beside me. He threw his arm around my shoulder and clicked on the television.

"What you wanna watch?"

"Oh, I think there's a Street Ball marathon on," I said eagerly.

"Nah, I'm not in the mood to watch basketball," said Percy as he clicked through the stations and landed on the nature channel.

So why ask me what I want to watch then? I wondered. And oh my gosh: Who the heck wants to see a deer get torn to pieces right before a meal?

"Um . . . I might lose my appetite watching this," I said coyly, hoping Percy wouldn't be offended. I wasn't used to being in a date-like situation with a new guy. Charles was my one and only boyfriend (if you could call him that) and we were free and easy with one another most of the time. I told Charles what I wanted straight up, and he did the same for me.

I didn't have that same vibe with Percy; then again, we were still brand-new.

Fortunately, Percy wasn't offended at all. He clicked off the TV, turned to me, and stared into my eyes. All I could do was stare back. Then he lifted my chin to raise my face with his pointer finger, and lightly touched the space between my right eyelid and eyebrow. *Oh brother, my scar.*

"How'd you get that?" he asked, frowning.

I really don't like bringing up my gangster past. But since Percy had already witnessed a part of it, I figured I might as well tell him the end of it. "Remember the gang I used to run with?"

"How could I forget?" Percy snorted.

"Well, when I got jumped out of the gang . . . Icy cut me."

"Oh man, that's terrible," he replied with knitted eyebrows.

"But I'm good," I said. "Other girls don't get to leave so easy."

"I always knew you didn't belong with those girls," said Percy. "And I always hoped you'd get out."

Percy's comment really touched me. Right then and there, I felt genuine concern for my well-being exuding from his pores. I can't even explain it . . . I felt such a powerful connection between us, like there was a magnetic force drawing us closer and closer together.

"And I promise you this," Percy continued, lightly tracing his finger over my scar. "I would *never* hurt you."

With these words, I suddenly thought back to how I had literally hurt him back in the day. Choked by guilt, I paused, and then spoke. "Well . . . I'm sorry for kicking you . . . you know where."

Percy chuckled. "Baby, you don't have to apologize to me. That was *years* ago. I'm fully healed. See?"

He grabbed my hand and acted like he was guiding me "there," but then he quickly switched it up (thank goodness) and guided my hand to his chest. "Can you feel my heart?" he asked. I nodded as I felt his heartbeat pounding rapidly through his shirt. "See? My heart's not broken. I'm good." He laughed at his own joke. I giggled, relieved that he didn't try to make me touch his stuff, and that he had accepted my apology so easily.

As nice as Percy was treating me, I couldn't help but feel bad, thinking back to how I had treated him and his mother. Even his arrogant mother didn't deserve the terror I used to set off in her store. Shoot, if Mrs. Thomas could give birth to a fine specimen like Percy, she couldn't be all *that* bad.

After a moment of silence, Percy's gaze flickered over my face, then my breasts, then my whole body. He started rubbing my neck, blowing his warm breath in my ear, turning me on like hot popcorn. I quickly relaxed under his spell. He slipped his tongue inside my mouth and kissed me so hard and passionately, like he was hungry for me, starving. His tongue was so delicious, so skilled, like a grown experienced man getting it *in*. Percy took complete control of my mouth.

"Mm, sweetheart," he moaned. "You feel so good."

Percy gently laid me down on the couch, and I sank into the leather. My body dissolved underneath him.

He hiked up my shirt, but the buzzer stopped him cold flat.

Pizza delivery saved me from some serious temptation.

When we finished eating, Percy tried me again. Kissing me all over, and feeling me up. This time, he went for my panties. "No," I said, and pushed his hand away.

Surprisingly, I only had to say it once.

"Okay, I can respect that," said Percy. He got up from on top of me and went into the bathroom. I fixed my clothes and thanked goodness he understood. A lot of guys think you being in the crib gives them the green light to get it. I felt so much admiration for Percy because he had actually respected my wishes without burying me in guilt. Now I was digging him more than before, if that was even possible.

We watched television for an hour, hugged up like a cute little couple. Then Percy turned to me and asked, "Are you having a good time?"

"For sure," I said. Shucks, I was cuddled next to a fine dude, far away from my group home. My guard was down and my spirits were up. Life was good.

Percy chuckled. "You said 'for sure' like a valley girl. It's supposed to be 'fo' sho." Are you sure you from Brooklyn? I'm saying, with a name like Kate, who you trying to fool?"

Ha, ha, very funny. People always got jokes about my plain-Jane name; but I've come to love my name, plain, and simple, because it's *mine*.

Oh, and by the way, wasn't Percy the one telling me how *pretty* my name was earlier? Now all of a sudden he was clowning on me?

I'd been trying to act extra mature around Percy, so I'd been holding back my playful side. But cracking back was long overdue. He had jokes? Shoot, I had jokes too. "Well, I never heard of a dude from *my* hood, or this *century*, named Percy!"

Percy's face grew serious. "I was named after my father. Please don't disrespect my father's name."

"Oh, sorry," I said.

Awkward.

Percy sat in silence for a couple of minutes. I felt like I wasn't sitting next to him. Like he was light years away. Finally, Percy came back down to earth and said, "I have a surprise for you. Let's go."

He jumped up from the couch, grabbed my hand, his keys, and we left the apartment. We headed down the brightly lit hallway and entered a dark stairwell. He led me up one flight of stairs, pushed open a heavy metal door, and boom, we were on the rooftop. There was a group of white people already up there, standing around talking with drinks in their hands. A few Asians, too. This was my first time being in an apartment building shared by other races. I felt worlds away from what I was used to. Percy didn't seem to know anyone, so he took me to a spot in the cut, away from everybody else. He guided me to the roof's ledge and stood behind me, hugging me. His arms felt so good wrapped tightly around me. I felt so wanted, so *needed.*

We had a clear view of the East River. Stars were sparkling in the sky. This was such a magical moment for me.

I didn't figure out that we were waiting for Macy's fireworks until the first burst of red, white, and blue pyrotechnics lit up the sky. "Wow," I exclaimed. "I've never seen fireworks up this close!" I looked up in awe at the breathtaking explosives crackling and popping over the ocean.

"See, baby, I can show you a whole lot if you let me," said Percy, hugging me. His hug was like a vise grip, so tight and intense, like he never wanted to let me go.

We watched the fireworks, hugging and kissing at intervals. Dazzling rainbows of light lit up the sky and my spirits, making me feel so alive inside. I had never experienced anything close to this magical moment.

This was a night wrapped in romance, Percy's lips so soft, gentle, and warm on my neck. I was overwhelmed. I didn't want the bliss to end.

But then I glanced at my watch. Ten o'clock curfew was looming over my head. Even though my group home was mad lax, I didn't want to take advantage of that. I turned to Percy and said, "Um, I have to go."

He looked disappointed. "Why?"

"I have to be back by ten," I said, and left it at that. I wasn't looking forward to explaining my foster care status.

"Where do you live?" asked Percy.

"Gravesend."

"Sounds depressing."

"Yeah, and you don't know the half," I blurted. That was all I planned to say.

"Well, let me clean up first; then I'll take you home."

I helped Percy clean up our earlier food mess, and then he grabbed the keys to the Avenger. While sitting in his car, I was busy thinking of an excuse for Percy to drop me off without seeing where I lived. I wasn't ready to let him fully inside my complicated life. The only guy I'd ever felt comfortable with knowing my personal business was Charles, because Charles had shared his own personal family drama with me many times before. . . . And speaking of Charles, oops; I had left my boy hanging!

As soon as I climbed into Percy's car, I turned to him and asked, "Can I use your phone for a quick second?"

"Sure," said Percy. He was about to hand me his BlackBerry, but when I whipped out the pamphlet from my pocket and started searching for Charles's scrawled number, Percy held on to his phone. He looked at me curiously. "I thought you were calling home." He jutted his chin toward the pamphlet. "You don't remember your own phone number?"

"No, I need to call my homeboy . . . I was supposed to braid his hair today."

Percy chuckled. "Oh, so you trying to call the *next* man on my phone? You got a lot of heart, shawty."

"He's just my homeboy," I repeated, not sure if Percy was kidding or not.

"Yeah, that's what they *all* say," said Percy, his head thrown back, laughter booming at his own joke. I still couldn't tell if Percy was seriously doubting my word, because he was laughing the whole time. But when the joke was over, and the laughter died down, he still didn't offer his phone. Maybe he forgot, I reasoned. So I just left it alone. Hopefully, Charles would understand.

Chapter 9

The closer we got to the group home, the more anxious I became.

"Can you drop me off at the corner of my block?" I suddenly thought to ask.

"But I want to see you safe inside," Percy protested.

"You can't," I said, shifting uncomfortably in my seat.

"Why?" he asked, with knitted eyebrows.

"Because."

"Because, why?"

It was dim inside the car, but I sensed confusion written all over Percy's face.

"What's wrong?" he asked, with concern in his voice.

Well, I wasn't about to lie about strict parents just to get him off my case. So boom. I caved in. Spilled my foster care story as if he had forced truth serum down my throat. Even sadder, I didn't stop there. I gushed about all my problems at the group home. My enemies, the dirty house, no privacy, no peace. When I finished blubbering, Percy reached for my hand and held it for a long time. "Sweetheart, nobody should have to go through all that," he said, wearing a sad expression.

I loved the way he called me "sweetheart," and I really appreciated his concern. I just stared at him with hope in my eyes, holding back my tears.

Percy finally let go of my hand and said, "So if the crib is strict like that, how can I stay in touch with you?"

I shrugged, dunno.

He leaned back in his seat, and said, "I'll figure something out." Then he reached for my hand again and rubbed it caringly.

I glanced at my watch. "I really have to go," I said, reluctantly.

"Well, when can I see you again?"

I wanted to ask if he was free tomorrow, but no, that would be too thirsty. "Is Wednesday good for you?"

"Wednesday is perfect," said Percy. "That's usually my day off."

"Where should we meet?"

"Give me a second to think." Percy caressed my arm with his warm, strong hands.

We sat in silent mode for five minutes straight. I know, because I kept peeking at my watch, feeling antsy about being late for curfew.

"Okay, I just thought of the perfect day for us," Percy exclaimed. "Do you know where the Atlantic Avenue Terminal is?"

"Yep."

"Can you meet me at the Starbucks inside the terminal at eleven AM?"

"Sure."

"Cool, then it's on," said Percy. "I'm going to show you a good time." He squeezed my hand tightly.

"Okay," I said, excited as ever. I had a second date with the man of my dreams. It couldn't get any better than this.

"All right, you better go now," said Percy. "Don't want you getting in trouble."

"True," I said, grabbing my gift bag from the backseat.

At the corner of my block, I jumped out of Percy's car, and waved good-bye, thinking he would peel off down the street. But Percy slowed his car to a crawl and tailed me to the group home's front door. At first, I felt apprehension, but the feeling quickly dissolved into appreciation. Percy cared. He really cared.

I swung open the front door, looked back at him and waved. Percy beeped twice, and the Avenger roared down the block.

Wow, the perfect gentleman, I marveled.

I walked—no, floated—into the house. I was hanging on cloud nine with Percy heavy on my mind. But as soon as I signed myself in, and went upstairs to my bedroom, I crashed right back down to earth.

Chapter 10

Oh. No. She. Didn't.

I stood frozen in my bedroom's doorway, staring at a disturbing sight: A new girl was sitting cozy on *my* bed with her back leaned up against *my* wall. She was a tall girl. Even sitting down, I could tell she had some height to her. She wore a tight yellow tank top and a light-blue mini jean skirt that barely covered her thighs. A smattering of red pimples covered her tan skin, and honey-brown hair flowed down her back. Her turquoise and pink Pastry sneakers hung over my bed, almost touching my doggone sheets. Pretty girl. But pretty bold. Her silly butt stretched all up in my spot, for what?

I glanced over at Tracy, who was sitting on her own bed, paying my presence no mind. Then I peeped a random twin bed squeezed into the far corner of our bedroom. I wondered why New Girl couldn't park her behind *there*, where it belonged. But then I quickly told myself: Kate, calm down, get a grip. I had no reason to trip. Technically, my bed was not *my* bed. Nothing is really your own in foster care. I been in this game long enough to know how it goes down: We run out of room. We get moved around and squeezed together like a can of freaking sardines. Tracy was already a problem. Now I simply had another one.

New Girl stared at me waiting for me to say something. But my tongue was stuck to the roof of my mouth.

"Kate, you can come in now," she finally said in a hoarse voice.

I hesitated.

"I don't bite," she added, wearing a smirk.

Since she knew me by name, I could already imagine what mess Tracy and crew been spittin' about me. Shoot, I was surprised New Girl even bothered to greet me in the first place.

"Hey," I said, awkwardly stepping inside the bedroom.

"I'm Jeselle," she offered, finally jumping up from my bed.

Tracy didn't say a word to me. At least she was keeping it real.

"Night staff is out like a light," said Jeselle. "We about to go out on the back porch and get twisted. You coming?"

Tracy sucked her teeth, swung her burgundy weave, and leaped from her bed. "I'mma be outside," she squeaked to Jeselle and bounced out the room.

"A'ight, ma," said Jeselle. Then she turned to me and asked, "So what you did for the Fourth? You got a man?" She jutted her chin toward my gift bag.

"I volunteered for a community garden," I said, wanting to add, "but I *might* have a man soon."

"Volunteering on a holiday?" Jeselle jerked her head back. "The hell made you do *that*?"

"My homegirl gave me the idea."

"Shoot, couldn't be me working for free . . . but good for you." Jeselle knitted her eyebrows and started shaking her head. "I didn't get to do anything today. Too busy getting kicked out my momma's house and moving here. My voice is mad froggy from yelling at her. She act so freakin' stupid sometimes . . . hitting me for no damn reason. She didn't think I'd hit her back this time. Well, she thought dead wrong."

I wasn't shocked by Jeselle's random confession; in foster care, you get used to the same sad stories volunteered out of nowhere.

Some girls don't care who they tell their stories to; they just want to get it out of their system, out into the open.

But since I didn't know Jeselle like that, I kept my mouth closed.

Jeselle unzipped the large black tote bag sitting beside her. "See, that's why I'm 'bout to sip me some Henny and get real relaxed. You coming?"

"Nah," I said, quickly leaving out the part about me being public enemy number one at the group home. I also left out the part that I don't drink anymore; somehow it always sounds like I'm trying to be high-and-mighty when it ain't even like that. It's like this: I get stupid when I drink, and I don't find vomiting and hangovers enjoyable, so I don't care what people think. I don't drink. Period.

But Jeselle seemed anxious to include me. "Aw see, I'm trying to toast to my new roomies." She jumped up and started singing, "Party, party, party, let's all get wasted!" Then she plopped back down on the bed, smiling at me, waiting for me to give in.

I wasn't about to. Instead, I decided to share a snippet of my situation. "Real talk, I don't get along with nobody up in here, so I'm not trying to get in where I *don't* fit in. Feel me?"

"Girl, don't let these crazy chicks intimidate you," said Jeselle, waving her hand in the air. She unearthed a big bottle of Hennessy from her bag. "Are you really gonna let them make you miss out on the good stuff, ma?" She put the bottle to her lips and pretended to sip. "Mm, mm, good!"

I cracked a smile, and then quickly grew serious. "Nah, I'm just not in the mood for nobody's bull right now."

"Now *that's* some bull," Jeselle teased.

"Nah, for real," I countered. "I already know what time it is. In my old group homes, I barely gave new girls a chance, either . . . now I'm getting it all back. . . . Karma ain't no joke."

Jeselle chuckled. "Yeah, I been in plenty group homes, too . . . used to boss them broads around like they was on my payroll. Girl, pimping wasn't easy!" She fanned her face and pretended to wipe invisible sweat from her forehead. I busted out laughing over her dramatics. Jeselle joined in at the sight of me cracking up.

Once our laughter died down, I thought, *Wow*, I don't even make friends this easy. In less than ten minutes, Jeselle had managed to defrost the icy wall I usually put up with new girls. Don't get me wrong: We weren't official homegirls yet, but there was something about her, something so real and upfront about her. I was impressed and cautious at the same time . . . you never know what folks are really up to. Only time would tell.

"Karma can't catch me here," said Jeselle, out of the blue.

"Yeah, I can see that," I replied. "You got Tracy on your team mad quick."

"Please, girl, Tracy and her goons knew they couldn't start none with me. I don't play that. Soon as I walked through the door they already knew. But they was talking mad smack about you, especially Tracy. I told them chicks straight to their face: I'm not trying to pick sides. I'm just here to do my time with no drama. I got enough drama at home."

"I feel you."

Jeselle held up her pointer finger and added, "If I don't work things out with my mother, then I only got one more year in the system. When I turn eighteen, I'm out of here . . . but hopefully, my mother will take me back."

"Why would you go back?" I wanted to ask. A mother physically fighting with her daughter is not a good look. But minding my own business, I simply said, "Five more years for me . . . and I don't have any family to go back to."

"Wow, that's tough," said Jeselle, as she dug in her bag again and unearthed a stack of plastic cups, followed by an empty orange knapsack. She stuffed the Henny bottle and the cups inside of the sack, hopped up from her bed, and headed toward the door. Before leaving, she stood at the doorway and said, "If you change your mind, come outside and get twisted with us."

"Okay," I replied. But *yeah right*, no, I wasn't.

I was already drunk with thoughts of Percy. He was still heavy on my mind. Had me floating on cloud nine. All I wanted to do was repeat the details of our romantic night in my head and then hit Replay all the way until the next day. Percy was so remarkably fine *and* kind. He made my night . . . maybe one day, my whole life.

Man, I was so hot for him. I needed to cool myself off with a shower. But no showers were allowed past ten. So I washed up real quick, threw on the pretty pink cotton nightgown Lynn bought me, climbed into bed, and pulled the sheets up to my neck. I drifted to sleep dreaming of Percy. I couldn't wait to see him again.

Chapter 11

On Wednesday, at eleven o'clock on the dot, I stepped inside of Starbucks, anxious and excited. Percy was already sitting at a table near the window, caught up in his BlackBerry. He didn't see me. So I decided to try my hand at flirting, since I was so brand-new at it. I snuck up behind him, and wrapped my arms around his neck. Bold of me, but hey, I wanted to step my girly game up.

Caught by surprise, Percy swiveled around in his chair, looked up at me, and his face broke out into a smile. He stuffed the BlackBerry in his back pocket. "Hey, baby," he said, then brushed my cheek with his soft lips, grabbed my hand, and we headed for the number 3 train. I walked tall with my handsome hottie by my side, proud as I could be.

While standing on the sweltering station's platform, Percy turned to me and said, "Sorry I couldn't pick you up in style, but parking in Manhattan is a pain, especially on a weekday."

"Oh, I don't mind," I replied, really meaning it. Shoot, I was just happy to be out and about with Percy, grateful that he was actually willing to rock me out in the streets. Most guys don't try to date you, they're too busy trying to *do* you; from day one, their main agenda is to get you to the crib and get the skins.

Percy was racking up so many points with me. And when we boarded the number 3 train, he racked up even more by asking, "So tell me, Kate, what's your favorite thing to do?"

Wow, what a guy, I thought. Percy was showing so much interest in getting to know me. Such a rare situation. My goodness! How could I not be impressed?

"Well, let's see. . . . I love basketball," I began, "and writing, and reading, and bugging out with my best friend, Felicia—"

"Whoa now," exclaimed Percy, in between chuckles. "I only asked for *one* thing."

I smiled, and thought to ask him the same question. It can't be all about me all the time.

Percy put his finger to his chin as if in deep thought and said, "Well, my favorite thing to do is . . . being with you."

"Aw," I said, beaming, "that was cute."

We got off the train at Chambers Street, and then waited for the number 1 to South Ferry. When the train finally came, Percy and I got on board, grinning up in each other's face. We continued grinning all the way until South Ferry, the last stop. Holding hands, we walked up what felt like a hundred flights of stairs, and made it out into the open air. The sun was shining, the weather was warm—what more could a girl ask for?

We walked toward a huge terminal where a bunch of people were flowing out.

"I hope there's not a long line," said Percy. "Don't want us to miss the next boat."

"Boat?" My eyes lit up. I hadn't even bothered to think about where Percy was taking me. I was just so happy to be with him. But now I was ecstatic. We were about to ride a boat! See the city sights! This was the kind of touristy thing Felicia and I used to do all the time—before Marlon came along.

We stepped inside the terminal. The line was perfectly short.

Five minutes later, we boarded a big white boat. Percy guided me to the railing, and stood behind me, holding my waist, as we sailed away from the pier.

"Ever heard of Governors Island?" he asked.

"Nope."

"It used to be a Coast Guard military base. Now it's like a public park."

"Wow," I said, feeling amped and giddy. I always wanted to do a date in the park. Now I was finally getting my chance.

"I was supposed to join the Marines last year," Percy suddenly volunteered. "But my mother needed help with the store." His face clouded over.

Oh no, here we go. His mother, again.

I always felt so torn when people complained about their parents. A part of me wanted to cuss them out for complaining, thinking at least they weren't discarded at birth the way my drug-addicted parents did me. The other part of me knew the sad truth: not every parent is meant to be. And sometimes you're better off *not* knowing who you come from. Blood ain't always thicker than water. Shoot, I'd take Ted, Lynn, Felicia, Tisha as my family any day; immerse myself in their *real* love instead of crying over fake blood.

In any case, who was I to judge? If Percy had to vent, let him vent. You never know what someone is going through until you're actually walking in their shoes. Percy looked so sad right now. It was amazing how the mere mention of his mother affected his mood so easily.

In an attempt to comfort him, I gently touched his arm, looked up into his beautiful light brown eyes, and said, "But if you had joined the Marines, I probably would have never had the chance to see you again."

A smile crept over Percy's lips. Instead of responding, he just gave me a hug, a big warm hug, and it felt so good. I loved how affectionate he was toward me. Percy didn't know how much I needed his affection right now. And I wasn't about to tell him. I was learning to keep some things to myself. Sometimes, boys use your confessions against you when thing go wrong. Percy didn't seem like the type to go sour on me, sweet as he was . . . but hey, you never know.

"Can you ride a bike?" asked Percy.

"Yeah . . . but I never owned one."

"Well, guess what we're about to do."

"Ride bikes?" I exclaimed. "Oh, that's what's up! I haven't ridden a bike in a minute." I was feeling so excited and antsy, like a five-year-old child.

As soon as we got off the boat, Percy made a beeline for a parking lot filled with a bunch of shiny blue and gold bikes. I was about to pick my own, but Percy said no, and pointed to a two-seater bike with a canopy on top. Oh, how cute.

"We can ride together," he explained. "I want you sitting right next to me." He winked at me. Like a shy doofus, I glanced downward, feeling all coy and girly. I swear, I wasn't used to this.

Percy paid for our two-seater, and off we went! The island was so picturesque; even with its abandoned brick buildings and occasional rocky pavement, there were so many hilly green lawns to admire throughout, so much history to learn about. We circled the whole perimeter of the island, taking our sweet time, talking, laughing, and pedaling away.

When we returned the bikes, our stomachs were audibly growling. We cracked up laughing, and started searching for food. Found a Jamaican lady selling good-smelling grub from her truck, which was parked on the grass.

Percy bought us a huge plate of rice, beans, baked chicken, and fried plantains. I couldn't wait to dig in. We went hunting for a spot to eat. Found a perfect picnic table under a perfect tree. Instead of sitting opposite me, Percy squeezed in right beside me, making sure our legs touched. He reminded me of Charles when he did that. But that's where the comparison ended. Percy was a perfect gentleman; Charles, a perfect player.

Percy handed me my fork, and we ate our food from the same plate. Such a romantic situation. I was self-conscious about my eating, though. Didn't want to be talking with my mouth full. Couldn't have any food stuck between my teeth. Everything Percy did was smooth and refined. I wanted to impress him, show him I had some class, too.

After lunch, we walked around the entire island. We stopped at a colonial house that had been turned into a museum, and admired all of the colorful artwork inside. Once outside, we sat down on a random bench, and Percy grabbed both of my hands and held them for a long time. "I'm having such a good time with you."

"Same here," I replied, staring into his magnetic light-brown eyes.

When it was time to leave, I didn't want to go. I wanted the boat to leave us behind, so we could be left alone on this beautiful island. This was the best day I had ever experienced in my whole entire life. And that's real talk.

"Thanks for taking me here," I said.

"Thanks for appreciating it."

Once on the boat, we stood in the same position as before, me leaning against the rails, Percy standing behind me, holding me close. I dissolved into his arms.

And when we rode the number 1 train, same idea, different position. His strong arms around my shoulders as I leaned up against his sexy chest.

When we were about to part ways, Percy asked, "Are you sure I can't call you at the group home?"

"Yeah, I'm sure."

It wasn't the staff or the bogus rules I was worried about. It was Makeba and her motley crew who would be blocking me from my potential boo.

Percy touched my shoulder and massaged it while saying, "But I need to stay in touch with you, sweetheart."

"I know," I replied, "I really wish things were different."

Percy paused in deep thought, heaved a big sigh, and then said, "Listen, stop by the store tomorrow at six o'clock. Wait for me across the street because I don't want my mom in my business. Can you do that for me?"

"Yes, I can," I said, feeling alive inside. Percy was really gunning to see me again. And the feeling was so mutual.

Percy leaned in and gave me a soft sensuous kiss on my awaiting lips. "I'm looking forward to next time."

"Me, too."

He grinned at me and said, "Yeah, I can see myself with you for a long, long time."

I timidly looked down at the sidewalk, stunned by the intensity Percy radiated inside my soul. He bent down to kiss me again. His kiss lingered on my lips all night long.

Chapter 12

As I waited for Percy across the street from his store, the powerful July sun beat down on me. I was hot as blazes, sweating through my t-shirt, feeling smothered by the humidity in the air.

I was a half hour early because I didn't want to be late, but I couldn't take the choking temperature much longer. I impatiently eyed the Fulton Street Market, wanting to run inside to escape the heat, but not while his batty mother was in the building.

Thankfully, at six o'clock on the dot, Percy emerged from the store. He was wearing a fresh white button-down short-sleeved shirt, beige linen shorts, and tan grown-man sandals. I didn't dig the sandals, but he looked really nice otherwise. Meanwhile, I was rocking a plain white T-shirt, baggy blue shorts, and my dollar-store flip-flops. Oh well.

Percy came across the street to greet me. He smiled slightly, hugged me tightly, and led me around the corner, away from his mother's line of sight.

Dead in the middle of the block, he stopped short, and started tonguing me down, taking me way off guard. He had given me no chance to even pop a mint! I hoped my breath wasn't kicking.

Guessed my breath was acceptable because Percy moved me up against the brick wall of an apartment building, and started getting at me again. Percy and I were acting out a love scene on the sidewalk. I melted into his strong arms, feeling so wanted, so needed, so happy to be with him. I was starving for his affection. A whole year of no hugs and kisses had me feeling deprived.

Now I was completely revived.

Percy finally released my waist and said, "I missed you."

I smiled at him, shyly. I didn't want to say "Missed you, too." This sounded too sappy for me. I needed some time getting used to this lovey-dovey stuff. Everything was happening so fast. But can I tell you? I was loving every minute of it.

Percy grabbed my hand and steered me farther down the block to his car. Once inside the Avenger, Percy pumped the air conditioner. The cold air felt so good blowing on my skin.

Percy turned to me and said, "I was hoping you'd wear something sexy. I wanted to take you out somewhere really nice today."

"Then why not let a girl know?" I *wanted* to say. But instead, I simply said, "Oh, I'm sorry."

Shucks, the concept of getting all dressed up to go on a date was straight-up foreign to me. Besides, I didn't think I needed to dress up. Percy was feeling me the last time he saw me in my simple-as-can-be outfit, so I assumed he'd be feeling me in a similar getup. My bad.

Percy was still looking disappointed when he said, "Anyway, I have something for you." He leaned over to open the glove compartment, and pulled out a shiny pink BlackBerry Pearl.

My eyes lit up like Christmas. "For me?" I asked, surprised out of my mind. "Are you sure?"

"It's nothing, sweetheart," said Percy, placing the phone in my hand. "My ex-girl's phone. All I had to do was turn it back on. She didn't appreciate it . . . but I know you will."

"Wow, thanks," I said, smiling so hard my cheeks hurt. I didn't think I'd own a celly till I turned eighteen. Percy was going hard for your girl, Kate!

Even though I'd already been warned that it's not good to accept early gifts from guys, I wasn't trying to give this phone back for nothing in the world. Call me stupid, call me crazy, but at least you could *call* me on my own phone for a change!

"Anytime you need me, I'm just a phone call away," said Percy.

Holla!

I happily toyed with the buttons of my new phone; it felt like gold in my hands. I couldn't wait to call Felicia with it. Now I would be able to talk to my homegirl outside of the group home without having some silly chicks breathing down my back. Shoot, I could dial my girl's number till my fingers turned black and blue.

"There's no data plan on the phone yet," Percy explained, "but if you behave, I'll add it for you later."

"So how do you make calls?" I asked.

Percy looked at me like I was an alien, took the phone, and showed me the basics. When I finally got a clue, he gave me back the phone. Then he gripped the steering wheel and gunned the engine. "Which train is better for you to get home?"

Hm, I had to think about that. The F train was better for me, but its closest station was miles away, in Downtown Brooklyn. I didn't expect Percy to drive me all the way downtown, so I told him the A train at Utica was fine.

"The A train goes to Gravesend?" he asked, with raised eyebrows.

"No, but I can transfer to the F train at Jay Street."

"Sweetheart, I asked which train is *better* for you," said Percy.

"The F . . . but that's way downtown," I explained. "I don't want to take you out of your way."

Percy chuckled. "You're sweet, but hardheaded. Did I *ask* you all that?"

"No."

"Okay then," he said, a bit abruptly.

"I was just trying to be helpful."

"And I appreciate that. As a matter of fact, I would've taken you all the way home if I could, but I just remembered I have to go handle some business." Percy paused for a moment, and then added, "But the next time I ask you a question, just give me a simple answer, okay?" Now, a bit of bass in his voice.

I was taken aback. There was no need for him to be getting snappy. Normally, if somebody snaps on me for no reason, I'm snapping back in under sixty seconds. But I didn't want the hard-core part of me to scare Percy away. I had already shown him how "Rocky" gets down, kicking him in the family jewels and whatnot. No doubt he *felt* the power of what I could do. So I wanted Percy to feel my softer side, the loving side of Kate. I finally had a man in my life who seemed to really care about me, so why should I ruin things over a silly misunderstanding?

"You catch the F at Jay Street, right?" asked Percy.

"Jay Street is perfect," I said.

Percy clicked on the radio. I sat in silence, looking out my window, a little pissed, but fighting the feeling.

As we cruised by Fulton Park, I spotted Charles posted up on the corner with his boys. I wanted to jump out the car to tell him sorry about Saturday, but I had a feeling Percy wouldn't like that. So I turned my head, and stared dead ahead.

When we pulled up in front of the Jay Street station, Percy boldly double-parked beside a police car. He jumped out the car, walked around it to open my door, and pulled me up out of my seat. Then he leaned me up against the back car door and wrapped me up into his arms. With his soft juicy lips, he planted a long juicy kiss. "Call me as soon as you get home," said Percy. "And don't let anybody see your new phone."

"I won't," I replied. I was way ahead of Percy in that regard, already planning a place to hide it. I trusted no one. Not even Jeselle. Been robbed in too many group homes to be letting my valuables hang loose.

As soon as I got home, I made a beeline for the bathroom. There was a cleaning cabinet, clearly not in use, with a bunch of stale cleaning products, buckets, and rags stuffed inside. Cool. I planned to stash my Blackberry there. Keep my phone in quiet mode, use a plastic soap storage box as a protective case, and then I'd wrap up the case in one of the rags. This tacky arrangement would have to do until I figured something else out.

Later that night, I checked my phone to see if Percy had called. Turned out, he had texted me three hours earlier. He must have hit me up as soon as he dropped me off at the train station. How very sweet and attentive of him, I thought.

I MISS YOU ALREADY.

MISS YOU TOO.

I WROTE YOU HOURS AGO. :(

SORRY. JUST GOT YOUR MESSAGE.

I WAS WORRIED ABOUT YOU. I TOLD YOU TO CALL ME.

SORRY, I DIDN'T GET THE CHANCE. BUT I'M OK. HOME SAFE.

GLAD YOU'RE OK. CAN'T WAIT TO SEE YOU AGAIN!

SAME HERE.

GNIGHT, BABY.

GNIGHT.

Chapter 13

On Friday evening, I was locked up in the bathroom, checking my phone. A text from Percy was waiting for me.

CAN I SEE YOU TOMORROW AT FIVE?

YES.

LOOK FLY FOR ME, BABY.

OKAY.

But, oh no! How could I look fly? I had no fly gear in my closet. Maybe some flies, but not any fly gear. What was a broke broad to do?

I flew out of the bathroom, and headed to my bedroom, gearing up to hunt for an outfit. But I stopped short at the sight of Mrs. Cooper, perched on the edge of my bed. My first thought was: Why is she still here? Her old butt should've *been* gone for the day.

"Kate, I need to see you in my office," she said.

My heart dropped down to my feet.

As I sat inside of Mrs. Cooper's cluttered office, wringing my hands, mad nervous, I wondered what the heck she wanted. The radio was pumping religious music. The fan sitting on her desk blew dusty air all over the place. I wished Mrs. Cooper would open the freaking window. Instead, she closed the door behind her. "Don't look so worried," she said with a raspy chuckle.

I flashed a nervous smile, nervous because random office visits never meant good news.

"Kate, I want you to know I've been thinking about your situation ever since you arrived," began Mrs. Cooper, holding a pencil to her mouth.

And?

"I understand you're on the fast track to success, while the girls here are . . . well, they could still use some guidance. The only reason you were placed here is because of a shortage of beds at another facility better suited for you."

My ears perked up. When, oh when, could I pack my bags?

"I just wanted you to know that you're at the top of the Green Hills' waiting list. They're expecting a free bed by September."

My high hopes dropped down to zero. Oh, come on now. Why would Mrs. Cooper call me into the office making grand announcements if the situation wasn't even set in stone yet? She must've read the extreme disappointment in my face because she added, "I see that you're having trouble fitting in with the other girls here. I just wanted to give you some good news to look forward to."

"Thanks," I muttered.

"In the meantime, is there anything I can do to make things better between you and the girls?"

"Yeah, kick everybody out the house," I wanted to suggest. Instead, I said, "That's okay. I'm good." Besides, Jeselle's presence was actually making things easier on me. Since all the girls were riding her bra strap, I could breeze by without beef because Jeselle had my back.

"Kate, you can't get through this alone," said Mrs. Cooper, fiddling with her lopsided Afro. She stared at me with sadness in her eyes.

Whatever.

It wasn't even that serious. My new thought process: Born alone.

Die alone. So what if the chicks here hated my guts? I've been through much worse. I could hold my own.

"I'm worried about you," said Mrs. Cooper, shaking her head.

"No need to." I shrugged. "But thanks, anyway."

Mrs. Cooper pointed the pencil at me and said, "Well, Green Hills is one of the best facilities in New York City. They'll help you with your independent living goals, and all of the girls there are on the same page as you, so it's a teamlike atmosphere. I'd be excited if I were you."

Well, you're not me.

Excitement refused to register on my face, because I'd learned a long time ago not to count on anything in foster care. Plans always change, and rarely for the better. No need for me to be doing cart-wheels just yet.

Mrs. Cooper babbled on and on about a few more "great" Green Hills details. But by this time, I was watching her mouth move with-out listening to a word she said.

I nodded at intervals with fake interest; all the while, I was thinking of my upcoming date with Percy, itching to bounce from the musty old office so I could head for my closet to hunt for some-thing decent to wear.

Mrs. Cooper tapped the desk with her pencil and said, "Do you mean to tell me I stayed after office hours to tell you the good news, and all I get is a blank stare?"

"I'm sorry," I replied. "I do appreciate you letting me know." I hoped this would be enough to zip the lady's lips. No disrespect, but she didn't know when to leave things alone.

Mrs. Cooper sighed at my response, and finally told me I could go. I thanked her, hopped out the chair, and flew out the door.

I stepped inside an empty bedroom, thanking goodness for some alone time. I started raiding my side of the closet for Operation Percy, only to resign myself to a plain shapeless white summer dress. It would have to do. Oh well.

After picking out my outfit, I had a whole hour to be by myself and bask in it. I really liked Jeselle, but she talked too dang much. And Tracy . . . well, you already know.

Unfortunately my peace was shattered at eight o'clock on the dot. Jesselle came busting inside the bedroom looking pissed to the tenth power. "Girl, you need to handle your business," she shouted. "Tracy trying to play you for a chump!"

"Huh, what?"

Jesselle plopped her butt on my bed, and shook her head. "All I'm saying, if I were you, I'd stomp Tracy out. Don't let her disrespect you no more. Stomp that girl out!"

Chapter 14

After Jesselle told me what had happened, stomping out Tracy didn't sound like such a bad idea. Apparently, earlier in the day, when I had gone to the store to buy me a pack of sunflower seeds, Tracy went shopping inside my knapsack. She had found my silver bracelet, threw it on her wrist, and rocked it right out the house. Jeselle saw the whole thing go down.

I hadn't noticed my bracelet was missing, because aside from my store run, I had stayed in the house all day. No reason to put it on.

"Wow," was all I could say, shaking with anger.

It was almost too hard to believe that Tracy could be that bold. Taking my bracelet in front of a witness? Really? A part of me was tempted to double-check my knapsack. But double-checking would be an insult to Jeselle. I had to believe her. And why would she lie?

Jeselle took off her sneakers and said, "Word to my mother, I wanted to wipe that stupid smirk off Tracy's face before she left the house. Reason I ain't do nothing is because I want *you* to do something. You too quiet around here and you gonna keep getting played for a punk if you don't stand up for yourself."

"Oh, I'm far from a punk," I said. "Trust."

"Well, that's not what I heard."

"I don't care what you heard," is what I wanted to say. But I didn't dare get smart with the only girl in the house who seemed to like me.

So I just sat still, quietly plotting on how to go about things in my head. Jeselle's only solution was a straight-up beat down. But nah; there had to be a better way. I turned to Jeselle and said, "See, I'm not trying to go backward for no silly broad. I came too far to go back there."

"Listen, if *you* can't handle her, *I* will," exclaimed Jesselle, still upset, as if the bracelet were hers.

"But I don't want you in some beef over me, because—"

"Listen," she interrupted, "if you can't handle her, I will."

"Nah, I'm good with my hands. I'm just trying not to go there—"

"Whatever," cut in Jeselle, clapping her hands with force. "I swear, I'm stepping to Tracy if you don't. Can't stand a thief. Wait until that girl gets home. Watch what I do."

Well, I didn't have to watch Jeselle do anything, because *I* did all the doing. It was time to show and prove that I could hold my own. And this is how it all went down.

I had calmly taken a seat on Jeselle's bed, peereing out the window every five minutes. Jeselle was sitting next to me, busy chattering away about nothing.

After the third time of Jeselle witnessing me peek outside, she finally thought to ask, "Why are you staking out our block?"

"You'll find out," I replied, with my forehead pressed against the windowpane.

Fifteen minutes later, I finally peeped Tracy walking up the street, alone.

"Guess it's time to put a chick in check," I said, jumping up from the bed. I raced down the steps two at a time. Jeselle was close at my heels. Night staff was nowhere to be found, and the other girls were missing in action. The perfect setting.

I flung open the front door with force.

Before Tracy could step over the threshold, I cut her off at the pass. Jeselle closed the door behind us. We stood on the porch, glaring at Tracy. "See what I'm saying?" Jeselle pointed to Tracy's arm.

Sure enough, Tracy had my beautiful silver bracelet on her wrist. I wondered if she was planning to rock it straight to my face, or was she planning to hide it before she stepped inside? Whatever the case, the sight of her brazenly wearing my property raised my temperature to boiling.

Tracy swung her weave bangs out of her face and said, "'Scuse me. Why y'all blocking me?"

"You real funny," I began. "Are you serious right now?" I wanted to hit her so bad my hands were shaking.

"What's the problem?" asked Tracy, like she really didn't know.

Real talk, the old me would've punched Tracy dead in the throat and yanked the bracelet off her wrist. The new me was trying to be civil about it.

"Take off my bracelet," I demanded, holding out my hand.

Tracy leaned her head to the side and said, "I'm saying, you be using up my perfume and stuff, but now I can't borrow your bracelet?"

"You didn't *ask* to borrow it," I snapped. "And you know full well I don't be using your stuff."

"*I* used your stuff," Jesselle piped in angrily. "Now what?"

Tracy stood her ground, not budging on the bracelet. So I got a little closer to intimidate her, although I was still determined to keep things nonviolent. My fighting days were supposed to be over.

"You better back up off me," said Tracy through gritted teeth.

"Then take off my bracelet . . . or do I have to take it off for you?"

Tracy looked over at Jesselle, and then at me.

"We not trying to jump you," blurted Jesselle. "I'm a fair fighter. So go 'head, Kate. Get it in!"

"Nah, I'm not trying to fight this broad," I explained. "She's not worth it. I just want my bracelet back."

My words must've sounded weak and spineless to Tracy because all of a sudden she got bold, raised her pointer finger to my face, and said, "I don't have time for this." Then she nudged me hard in the forehead. To top off her nerve, she turned her back on me, thinking I was too much of a punk to check her. I lost it then and there.

"You must be out your mind, trick!" I grabbed a handful of her weave, wrapped her hair around my wrist, and yanked her head straight back. While my left hand gripped the hair, my right hand balled into a fist and connected with her face, full force. Tracy almost dropped from the blow. But I held her up by her hair and was about to pound the girl to death.

"I'll kill you," she yelled, crying and spinning her arms at the empty air in front of her.

I let go of her hair and effortlessly tripped her to the ground. My fists were cocked and ready to launch. I wanted to stomp Tracy out. But something inside me stopped me cold flat. I was overdoing it. In actuality, all I wanted was my bracelet back. So I sat on her stomach, grabbed her right arm, and yanked my prized possession off her chubby wrist.

"We could've done this the easy way," I said, out of breath.

Jeselle stood behind me laughing her head off. "Dang, Kate, that was quick. I didn't know you could get down like *that*!"

The next day, everybody but the staff knew how I got down. Jeselle had bragged about my fighting skills all day, like a proud parent. Now the girls were steering clear of me. They knew what I could do, and they didn't want to get *done*.

Tracy avoided eye contact with me the whole time at the breakfast table. I felt so bad seeing the nasty bruise splotched on her dark brown skin, looking like permanent purple Magic Marker. It was easy to see that she had gotten clocked in the face; nothing else could explain the damage. But the no-snitching rule held mad weight in our house. So Tracy blamed the bruise on a fight during her home visit. Then she bounced from the crib immediately after breakfast, scared straight, I guessed.

Although I didn't get punished for my actions, I still felt troubled. Troubled because when you have the kind of life I have, it's so easy to get sucked back into violent mode. I couldn't believe that I had risked everything over a bracelet that could be replaced. Tracy's life couldn't be replaced if I killed her from a freak accident, a fatal punch gone wrong—you never know. And as angry as I was last night, that's what I could've done.

The longer I thought about it, the sicker to my stomach I felt. I replayed the fight over and over in my head, so mad at myself for not handling things differently.

But soon, enough was enough. I did what I did, and hopefully I wouldn't have to do it again. I pushed the incident way in the back of my mind, and forced myself to push pleasant thoughts in the forefront, namely thoughts about Percy. I thought about his sexy lips, his sensuous kiss. Thoughts of him easily relaxed my mind.

Then it suddenly hit me. I *shouldn*'t be so relaxed when it came to my appearance; Percy was too special for a shapeless summer dress. What in the world was I thinking? What was I going to wear? Saturday was less than twenty-four hours away!

I tore up my side of the closet again, hunting for something decent. Nothing. I had absolutely nothing. I badgered my brain trying to think of a solution. Couldn't think of a doggone thing. Our allowance was so sorry; a few dollars a week couldn't buy me *jack.* And none of these broads would let me borrow their clothes. Please, I wasn't foolish enough to ask any of them. Then again, Jeselle was crazy cool and would most definitely hook me up. Too bad she was taller than a tree; nothing of hers would fit me—

See . . . that's why I wished things were different around the house. Tracy is a shorty like me, in fact, my *exact* body type. Why couldn't we be were more like sisters instead of stone-cold enemies, fighting and beefing over nonsense? Imagine how dope it would be if we could share one another's clothes and secrets, getting along with each other like one big happy family. That's all I ever wanted was a family . . . but anyway. No need to get off track. I had to bring my mind back to Percy.

I had disappointed my dream boy once already, looking like a straight-up cornball last time I saw him. There was no way on Earth I was going to disappoint him again.

Chapter 15

Early Saturday morning, I jumped out of bed with a single hopeful thought swirling through my head: Felicia. Felicia might be able to save my day!

Back in June, Felicia had mentioned a yellow stretch dress she had bought for one of her countless dates with Marlon, but ended up not wearing it.

"OMG, the lycra emphasizes my lanky bones," Felicia had complained. "I don't look sexy. I look anorexic!"

"Aww, poor anorexic baby," I replied, forcing a laugh. At the time, I was depressed about leaving the Johnsons and trying to hide it behind a jokey façade.

"One size fits all, my behind!" Felicia continued.

"What behind?" I teased. "I thought you didn't have one."

"Well, you definitely have the curves to do this dress justice," explained Felicia. "You can come get it whenever you want."

At that time, I was too busy moping to be thinking about a dress. So I told her I would come, but never did. I had no reason to.

Fast-forward to today. Now, I had a purpose. A hot, hot date, and I couldn't wait! I hoped Felicia hadn't given my dress away.

I took my shower, hopped into any old thing, and ran out the house with my BlackBerry stuffed inside the pocket of my jeans. I walked two blocks to a small park, sat on a bench, and dialed Felicia with anxious fingers.

"Hey, Fee, welcome back, sorry for calling you so early, but I need a big favor."

"Wow, you said a mouthful," exclaimed Felicia. "What's up?"

"Do you still have that yellow dress you wanted to give me?"

"Yep. It's still in a bag waiting for you."

"Oh man, thank you so much!" I sighed with relief. "What's the earliest I can come through?"

"Anytime you want. I have to get ready soon anyway. Marlon's been whining about missing me all week, so he's coming over for breakfast. My mom is making us a serious spread . . . of course you're welcome to join us."

"Oh, no thanks," I said quickly.

I couldn't stand Felicia's parents, both big-time lawyers who held their noses too high, not a down-to-earth bone in their bodies. In the projects is where Felicia's parents first met, but they were steady trying to forget, acting all stiff and superior over others. I could tell they didn't really approve of my friendship with Felicia. And the only reason they tolerated me was because I rocked good grades and was the first *real* friend Felicia ever had.

"What number are you calling me from by the way?" asked Felicia.

"It's a surprise," I replied. "Anyway, I'll be there around eleven," I added, hoping they'd be done with breakfast by then.

"Okay, and don't think I forgot, Ms. Thing," began Felicia. "I *will* be grilling you about your new man!"

I giggled, feeling all girlish and giddy. I couldn't wait to be grilled.

At eleven o'clock on the dot, I landed on Felicia's spic-and-span front porch, and rang her bell. Her house was the best on the block, a flawless brownstone painted peach on top and dark brown at the bottom, a shiny black gate, not a crumbling step or chipped stone in sight. Even her garbage cans sat there all prim and proper.

Felicia flung open the door, and greeted me with a big hug. "What took you so long?" she asked, playfully.

"Shoot, I ran all the way here," I joked.

As soon as I walked through the front door, the delicious aroma of bacon, waffles, and coffee wafted in the air. The kitchen was miles away from their brightly lit hallway, but the smell of good food was overpowering me. "Dang, Kate, you be tripping," said my stomach, resenting my foolish pride.

"Come say hi to everybody." Felicia led me into the kitchen.

I reluctantly followed.

Felicia's kitchen was all glossy wood and tiles shining, and in it sat Felicia's beefy, bespectacled father, her skinny serious-faced mother, and Marlon. Their oak kitchen table was huge, but Marlon was sitting right up under Mrs. Coldwell, already looking like part of the family. Felicia's father sat opposite them, with *The New York Times* raised up to his face. I got a quick hello from everyone.

Then Marlon continued where he had left off. "My mom may be a chef, but she can certainly take lessons from you, Mrs. Coldwell."

Oh, what a brown nose, I thought; but I wasn't mad at Marlon. You gotta do what you gotta do to get in good with the parents!

Mrs. Coldwell gave a fake, restrained laugh, and she patted Marlon's shoulder. "You're too sweet."

Felicia beamed at the scene.

"So, how are things with you, Kate?" asked Mrs. Coldwell.

I put on my proper voice and replied, "Everything is fine, thank you."

By now, I was fidgeting. I wanted to get my dress and be out. So I turned to Felicia and said, "Sorry, but I really can't stay long."

I was glad Felicia got the hint. She told everyone, "Be right back," and led me up the polished wooden steps into her colossal bedroom. This year, her walls were painted lavender, a new plush purple comforter covered her canopy bed, and lacy cream curtains adorned the room's huge windows. Before stepping fully inside, I slipped off my sneakers. Then I plopped down on her bed and ran my feet through her lavish cream carpet.

Felicia plopped down next to me and exclaimed, "OMG! So tell me more about Percy. Where'd you meet him? How old is he? Why haven't you mentioned him to me before the festival?"

"Whoa, slow down," I said, laughing. "You got twenty-one questions!"

"Can't help myself," exclaimed Felicia, giggling. "Percy is definitely a cutie-pie!"

"I know, right?" I beamed. "He's really feeling me, too. He can't keep his hands off me—"

Just as I was about to give Felicia the full scoop, my cell phone rang. This was such a proud moment. I coolly whipped out my pink BlackBerry Pearl from my pocket, all smooth and cool. Yes, your girl, Kate, was flossing with her Pearl. I checked Felicia's reaction from the corner of my eye, but I couldn't tell what she was thinking.

"Hey, baby," said Percy in his sexy deep voice. "How you doing?"

"I'm good," I replied, smiling.

"Where are you?" he asked.

"Felicia's house."

"Who, Miss Africa?" Percy laughed. I chortled, uncomfortably. Felicia was sitting right next to me and could probably hear him. So I got up and walked over to the window, pretending to look outside.

"Listen, change of plans for today," Percy began. "One of our customers sold me last-minute tickets for a Broadway play called *King of Pride*. We have to be in Manhattan by two o'clock. Can you be ready in time?"

"Sure," I exclaimed. Wow, this would be my first Broadway play ever. Percy was really going hard for me!

"Right now I'm downtown running errands for my mother," explained Percy. "So can you meet me in front of Macy's by one o'clock?"

"No problem," I said, without thinking about all I had to get done, namely my hair. My cornbraids were mad frizzy, and I didn't have time to go all the way back to the group home to fix it. But even that fact couldn't lessen my excitement.

"I can't wait to see you, sweetheart," said Percy.

"Same here," I replied.

I hung up the phone, grinning, my heart fluttering. So many times I had to overhear Marlon talking sweet nothings to Felicia, while I had nothing. Now I had *something*, a real relationship. I was finally someone else's sweetheart, and I was going to see a Broadway play with that someone, a special someone I never dreamed I could get.

Before I could turn from the window, I felt Felicia's breath on my neck.

"Wow, cool phone," she said, her eyes mad wide.

"Thanks." I beamed. "Percy gave it to me."

Felicia's eyebrows twitched, and she paused before saying, "Oh . . . that's nice."

"What's wrong?" I asked.

"Nothing," said Felicia, averting her eyes.

"But your whole attitude just changed," I insisted.

"I said nothing's wrong."

I twisted my lips to the side, which was my yeah-right look. "Felicia, come on now. How long have I known you? Why are you fronting? Tell me why your whole face just changed. What's the matter?"

Real talk, Felicia was ruining my moment. My agenda was supposed to be: give her the scoop about my two magical dates with Percy, get my dress, thank her profusely, and be out.

But now this.

I refused to leave Felicia's crib without making sure she was okay. Point-blank, period, I had to know what was up.

"Do I ever hold back on you?" I asked, growing frustrated.

"Kate, please don't press me," Felicia pleaded. "Nothing is wrong. I swear."

Whatever.

When you're really tight with someone, they can lie with all their might, and you can still see right through them.

"Spill it, Felicia," I insisted. "Don't have all day."

Felicia heaved a big sigh and said, "Okay, since you asked for it." She couldn't even look at me when she began to explain. "I don't mean any harm . . . but isn't it too soon for Percy to be giving you a phone . . . an expensive phone at that?"

Oh, is that all?

"It's not a new phone," I quickly explained. I walked over to Felicia's bed and plopped down to put my sneakers back on. I was gearing up to go, even though I could tell Felicia had some more nonsense to say.

"Kate, don't you think it's too soon to be giving out phones, period? I mean, Percy seems like a really nice guy, but you've only known him for what . . . a week or two?"

"Hi, hater," I said, half-jokingly.

"I'm not hating," Felicia objected. "Just concerned."

"Concerned about what?" I asked, cocking my head to the side.

"Well, the only reason I know a guy to give a girl a phone so soon is to keep track of her . . . I mean, you *just* met the guy."

"Not true," I corrected. "Percy and I have known each other for years. Besides, like I said, it's not even a new phone. So please relax." I chuckled, trying to keep the mood light.

"Okay, let me mind my business. . . . It's just that . . . well, you know my mom is a prosecutor . . . and I hear a lot of stories."

"Yeah, okay, I feel you," I said.

I had to admit, Percy *was* spending money on me mad quick. But he was holding down a job, his parents were paid, so I knew he wasn't hurting for cash. Shoot, at least I didn't have to sleep with him to get mine.

And how *else* was Percy supposed to stay in touch with me if he didn't give me this BlackBerry? Felicia knew the group home drama I had going on, so why was she acting brand-new?

Besides, Tisha was the main one forever lecturing me about knowing that I deserve the best in life. So why should I question all this good stuff I was finally getting? Why not appreciate the gift-giving while it lasted?

"Just be careful," said Felicia. "That's all I'm saying."

"Yeah, yeah, I feel you," I said, growing antsy. I had no time for lectures. I had things to do.

I *been* ready to bounce. But then I suddenly remembered: my dress. So I kept my butt planted on the bed, regreting that I had to depend on someone else for my gear; it was the same sad story last year. My ex-friend Naleejah had treated me like a straight-up charity case, and had reminded me about my sorry hand-me-down existence to a whole audience's face. Although Felicia would never do me like *that*, my clothing dependency was still whack. Right then and there, I vowed to start earlier on my summer job hunt next year, so I would have some real paper in my pocket to buy my own dang clothes for a change.

"Well, Percy definitely is a cutie-pie," said Felicia, as an afterthought. Probably trying to make me feel better.

"Isn't he, though?" I said. "So um, can I get my dress now?"

"Where are you guys headed?" she asked, still forcing an unconcerned air.

"Um, Percy says it's a surprise," I fibbed. If Felicia was already questioning my phone, why would I fix my mouth to tell her about a Broadway play?

Felicia moseyed over to her walk-in closet and pulled out a small red shopping bag. I took the bag and said, "You really saved me, girl. Good looking out . . ."

Then my voice trailed off. I suddenly realized I needed shoes, too. Couldn't rock my raggedy sneakers with a banging stretch dress.

Felicia's feet are way bigger than mine so I couldn't borrow her boats. The only other choice was to ask for a loan, something I had never in my life done before; my pride had never let me . . . until now. "Um, Felicia, can you lend me a twenty until Friday?"

Felicia opened her brown eyes wide, clearly shocked. As many times as she tried to push cash on me, even in my neediest times, I've always said no . . . so I could see why she was stunned.

"Is everything okay, Kate?"

"Everything's fine," I said. "I just forgot my money at home, and I need to pick up a few things. Don't worry, I promise to pay you back on Friday."

Felicia tapped my arm. "Stop playing, you know I trust you. I just can't believe you're finally asking. How many times have I told you that you never have to go without as long as you have me?"

"Aw, thanks girl," I said.

Felicia walked over to her shiny cherrywood desk, and pulled out her wallet from the top drawer. She handed me the twenty. But I felt like she still had some unexpressed Percy questions. So it was time to make my exit. Quick.

"Well . . . Marlon is probably missing you," I said.

"Oh . . . okay."

Felicia's demeanor was still funny-style. I couldn't believe she was still concerned over a silly phone. Because really? It wasn't that serious. And honestly, I couldn't care less what she thought. I was ecstatic about my new phone and my new man, and I didn't want anybody bringing me down.

Felicia followed me downstairs. I poked my head into the kitchen and said my good-byes. Once outside, Felicia leaned against her door's frame and said, "Have a nice time."

"Thanks, girl," I called over my shoulder. "I will!"

I ran all the way to the Utica Avenue train station, and was still catching my breath when the A train pulled in.

On the train, I plotted my action plan. First, I was going to run to the beauty store to buy some gel and a cheap scarf to press down the frizz in my cornbraids real quick. Then I was going to find some decent-looking sandals for under fifteen dollars.

However, as soon as I made it out of the Jay Street train station, I ended up stumbling upon a random discount-shoe store. I bought a pair of average black open-toe sandals. Planned to buy gel and scarf next. But then I checked my Blackberry and discovered it was fifteen minutes to one.

Oops, no time for that! I flew inside Macy's third-floor bathroom, slipped into my sexy dress, my sandals, and then, with horror, stared into the mirror at my fuzzy head of hair. I already knew it was bad, but the bright light emphasized the fright. Nothing I could do, though. There was no time. In a panic, I rushed outside to meet Percy.

Chapter 16

I dashed up to my post in front of Macy's, and waited for Percy. At one o'clock on the dot, he strolled up to me, looking gorgeous. His hair was cut close to his perfectly shaped head, and his edges were lined up with precision. He wore a navy-blue short-sleeved polo shirt, baggy beige shorts, and tan grown-man sandals. His vanilla-almond skin glistened in the sun. First thing he said to me, "Wow, sweetheart, you look really good . . . but why didn't you fix your hair?"

"Yeah, I know," I stuttered, "but you didn't give me enough time to get ready."

"Oh, so it's my fault?" Percy asked with raised eyebrows.

"No, no, I'm not saying that—"

"Forget it," interrupted Percy.

Without grabbing my hand like he usually did, Percy started walking down the block and expected me to follow. Meanwhile, dudes on all sides of me had their tongues wagging out their mouths at the sight of my curvaceous body sheathed in yellow stretch material—fuzzy hair and all. Maybe Percy suddenly realized this, because halfway down the block, he finally reached for my hand. When we got to his car, he held the car door open for me.

Back to being a gentleman, thank you very much.

During the ride to Manhattan, Percy was quiet. The radio was pumping loud bass-driven beats. I just sat back in my seat, enjoying the view of the busy streets, and then the Brooklyn Bridge, vowing to one day walk over it, hopefully with Percy.

We made it to the theater in record time. I stared up at the brightly lit marquee for the *King of Pride*, and started getting excited. When we got inside the theater, I was bowled over by everything. I stared in awe at the huge glittering crystal chandeliers, hundreds of red seats in neat rows, and fancy-looking folks mixed in with casually dressed people.

"I lucked up getting these tickets," said Percy, out of the blue.

"I'm glad you did," I exclaimed. "This is my first Broadway play."

"Yeah, I can tell," said Percy.

The usher showed us to our seats and handed us our playbills. I already planned to put my playbill straight into my Lifebook's inner fold. This was such an exquisite experience, I needed to preserve it.

We sat in the middle row, close enough to see the full stage. My mouth dropped open as soon as the curtains parted, revealing a breathtaking backdrop painted bright red, orange, and cobalt blue. Tribal beats filled the theater and huge puppets and people in masks began running across the stage, dancing and singing all over the place. One magical scene flowed into the next. By the time the show was over, I was close to tears. It was such an amazing experience. I wanted to yell out, "Encore, I want more!" But I didn't dare. Percy would probably not approve.

Once outside of the theater, he turned to me and asked, "Enjoyed the show?"

"Big-time," I exclaimed. "Thanks for taking me . . . wow."

"You hungry?"

"For sure," I said.

We were walking down Forty-second Street and Percy stopped short in front of McDonald's. "I would take you somewhere much nicer to eat, but I have to rush back to the store. My mother's doing inventory today, of all days." Now he looked pissed.

"I'm not mad at McDonald's," I said, trying to cheer him up. "Love me some French fries!"

We stepped inside McDonald's, and I had to double-check the double arches on the cashiers' shirts because I had never been in such a clean and fancy fast-food restaurant in my life. I was surrounded by nice brick walls and dim lighting and computers lined up to my right. "This is the baddest Mickey D's I've ever been in," I exclaimed.

"Please, this is nothing," he replied. "I'll show you a *real* fancy restaurant . . . one day."

Without asking me what I wanted, Percy placed two orders of McNuggets and fries. I asked him to add a hot chocolate to the order. "Hot chocolate in the summer time?" he exclaimed.

"I have a taste for it. Love me some hot chocolate," I said, giggling.

But I stopped giggling when he ordered me fruit punch instead.

No reason to beef about it, especially not after my beautiful Broadway treat, so I ate my food, and drank my punch with a smile.

Percy finished eating before me. He pushed back his chair and got up before I was through eating my last few fries; I gobbled them down and got up, too.

His car was parked on Fortieth Street, close to Bryant Park.

"It's a nice day, let's sit in the park for a few minutes," said Percy.

He grabbed my hand and led me across the street. There was a huge fountain in front of us spewing water. People sat all around us, reading newspapers, lying out to get some sun, and just plain old chilling. Percy pushed two green chairs together and made us a bootleg loveseat. We faced the huge lawn and he wrapped his arm around me, stroking my shoulder with his warm hand. No words were exchanged, but it was such a romantic moment, a moment that unfortunately had to end way too quick.

"I have to head back," Percy said with a sigh.

"Well, I had a really nice time."

"Me, too, sweetheart," said Percy. "I love being around you. You make me happy."

I went to bed dreaming of Percy; and woke up in the middle of the night scared to death. First, I heard Jeselle's voice. Then I opened my eyes to the sight of someone climbing through our window. I sat up in bed with a jolt.

My eyes adjusted to the darkness. I realized it was just Tracy.

"We forgot to tell you," whispered Jeselle, "got us a new system. If you want to stay out overnight with your man, just let us know and we got you."

Jeselle explained the system, the fake body in the bed, and the window tap. Tracy and I still weren't on full speaking terms, but having one another's back in sneaky situations was customary in most group homes. It's usually "us" against "staff," so we had to look out for each other no matter what.

I almost busted out laughing when Tracy uncovered the two large plastic bags full of clothes that was supposed to be her body. I had never seen this brand of trickery before. Reminded me of a jailbreak plot.

Later that day, I said to Jeselle. "Shoot, as long as Belinda and Gerald work here, it seems like we don't even have to go through all that body-bag stuff. We can just walk straight through the front door any time of day. They don't care."

Jeselle waved her hand to dismiss my comment. "Nah, girl, we can't be doing things straight to their face. That would be disrespectful."

"But batty Belinda barely makes the rounds for head counts," I joked. "Does she even have a brain inside her head?"

"Yeah, but the body-bag trick is better than nothing," Jeselle insisted.

Meanwhile, I was thinking how I might be needing a body bag soon. Percy had hinted that he wanted me to spend the night with him. This is something I would have never considered if Common Grounds was a normal group home. But since staff was such a big joke here, why not go for broke in order to please my man?

Chapter 17

I WANT TO SEE YOU, BABY. I MISS YOU.

I MISS YOU TOO.

CAN YOU COME OVER MY FATHER'S HOUSE TODAY?

YES.

COOL. MEET ME AT JAY STREET. SAME SPOT. SIX O'CLOCK.

OKAY.

My Friday was all set. First, I had to pay Felicia back her money as promised. Then, I had to see my baby. Since Felicia and Marlon already had movie plans at the Court Street Theater, I would be able to kill two birds with one stone. The theater was only a few blocks from where I had to meet Percy. So first stop, the theater.

Felicia and Marlon were standing outside waiting for me, dressed like twins again: identical purple T-shirts, and blue jean shorts. So corny and cute of them. "Y'all are too much," I laughed, handing Felicia a crispy twenty-dollar bill.

"Oh goody," she exclaimed. "Now we can get some extra popcorn, Marlon!"

I chuckled at how Felicia loved to play off her wealth. Homegirl could buy a hundred bags of popcorn if she really wanted to. But no one would ever guess from the raggedy way she dressed. I admired her humbleness, though. So many kids in the hood be dressing too good with no money in the bank. I'd rather be rich and raggedy than fly and faking it. Who do I need to impress? Well, maybe Percy. . . .

"Kate, you should come with us," said Marlon.

I smirked at the idea. I knew he wasn't joking because I'd been invited to go to the movies with them in the past. But now that I had Percy in my life, I didn't feel so pitiful over his suggestion this time.

"I would love to join y'all," I began, "but I'm meeting Percy in a few."

As soon as I said this, my BlackBerry buzzed in my pocket. Amazing, I thought, just look at how strongly I was connected to my baby!

"Hey, sweetheart," Percy began, "I'm here earlier than expected. Where are you?"

"Court Street."

"Court Street?" he repeated. "How far away from Jay Street?"

"A few blocks away . . . I'm in front of the movie theater."

Guessing it was Percy, Marlon tapped me on the shoulder. "You guys should join us. Ask him!"

"Who's that?" asked Percy, with sudden bass in his voice.

"Marlon," I said, taken aback by Percy's tone.

"Who?"

"Marlon," I repeated. "Um . . . you remember. . . . You met him at the African Festival . . . Felicia's boyfriend . . . and she's here, too."

"But why are you there with them, when you're supposed to be meeting me?"

"Because I didn't expect you to be ready until six."

Percy paused and then said, "Well, I'm ready now. Are you?"

"Yes, I'm ready," I said. "I only had to drop something off real quick," I added, defensively. I wanted to snap on Percy for snapping on me, but I couldn't; I had an audience.

"Well, I'm coming to pick you up," said Percy. "Wait for me there."

"Okay," I said, feeling funny, and hoping it didn't show in my face.

I glanced at Felicia. Her face looked just as funny. Knowing my homegirl, I already felt her "concern." The fact that I had to explain myself to Percy clearly didn't sit right with her.

Marlon was either playing it off, or didn't have a clue, because he said, "We should really do the double-date thing soon, though. So let's make it happen, Kate!"

I forced a chuckle. Then Felicia had the nerve to say, "I doubt that she can."

"You doubt *what?*" I asked, with an attitude.

Felicia had nothing to say.

Yeah, you better zip it, chick.

There was no need for Felicia to be a smart aleck about my relationship in front of Marlon. This was exactly why I had avoided calling her smart-alecky-butt all week. I knew if I spoke to her too soon, I'd end up slipping about the Broadway play, and she'd end up lecturing me about "early" gifts. I didn't need her in my ear flapping her gums about nothing.

Don't get me wrong. I appreciated Felicia's concern—whether valid or not—but she was really overdoing it right now, eyebrows raised, all dramatic for no reason.

Marlon checked his watch and told Felicia, "Listen, if you want to get popcorn, we better go."

"True," said Felicia. "Talk to you later, Kate." She gave me a stiff hug good-bye. Then Marlon hugged me, too, and they went inside the theater arm in arm. Five minutes later, Percy pulled up to the curb. I hopped inside his car.

"So where's your friends?" he asked, in a suspicious tone.

"They had to leave." I fidgeted in my seat.

"So soon?"

"Their movie was about to start," I explained. Honestly, I didn't appreciate Percy's line of questioning, but I wanted to keep an open mind about it. Come to think of it, If I called Percy and heard a female's voice in the background, I'd probably be tripping, too.

"I can call Felicia if you like," I volunteered, hoping he'd say no.

"But did I *ask* you to call her?"

"No."

"Okay then."

Percy peeled down Court Street. He hopped onto Atlantic Avenue, and started driving like a madman.

By the time we got to his father's house, I was not in the best of moods. So when he laid me on the couch, trying to go for my drawers, I told him no with so much firmness in my voice.

"Why?" he asked, still tugging at the elastic of my thong.

"I'm not ready," I said.

"But if two people are feeling each other, the natural thing to do is to make love."

"Yeah, I hear you, but fall back," I wanted to say. Instead, I just lay there quietly, pushing his hand away every time he tried me. This was such a drag. Maybe we needed to do more outdoorsy activities. Oh well, I thought, what a letdown.

Percy finally sat up on the couch, clearly pissed. He wouldn't talk to me. And I'm no dentist; I wasn't about to pull teeth. Besides, what happened to the guy who told me he respected my wishes when he had tried me last time? This was a different Percy; I wanted the other one back.

"Maybe I should go home," I said, sadly.

"Yeah, maybe you should." Percy jumped up from the couch, grabbed his car keys, and drove me to the F train instead of all the way home. Not a problem for me. It was only eight o'clock, a nice warm summer night, and during my walk home from the train station, I had some time to think. Told my Lifebook all about my thoughts.

My relationship with Percy is starting to feel like a roller-coaster ride. My stomach dips and flips at the thought of disappointing him. Why was he so huffy over me not wanting to have sex with him yet? He claimed he can see himself with me for a long time, so what's his rush? If Percy expects to get my treasure, then he needs to start treating me like gold, all of the time, not just some of the time. I may be new at this relationship stuff, but I have to stay true to myself, no matter what.

Chapter 18

CAN I SEE YOU TODAY?

I read Percy's text, scowling. I was still upset about yesterday. I sat on the tub's edge, glaring at the screen of my phone.

Then he texted me again, a split second later.

I WANT TO TAKE YOU OUT SOMEWHERE SPECIAL, BABY. PLEASE?

Baby?

Please.

Percy was still getting no answer from me. I couldn't believe his utter flipping nerve. He had practically kicked me out of his father's house for not giving him any sex, making me feel like a defected object he could no longer use, and yet, here he was, texting me like nothing happened? True, I was the one who had suggested me leaving, but he didn't have to jump at the chance to show me the dang door.

I'M REALLY SORRY ABOUT YESTERDAY.

Okay, finally, a "sorry." At least now he was showing me some accountability. However, hold up. Sorry or not, I was still wondering if I should even respond to Percy.

But before I could make up my mind, my phone vibrated in my hand. Percy's name lit up in lights. I answered in a lackluster voice.

"Hello?"

"Hey, sweetheart, did you get my texts?"

"Yes, all three of them," I said, sarcastically. I couldn't help myself. Nobody craps on Kate without repercussions.

"Well . . . I wanted to say this to you over the phone, instead of a text. . . . I'm sorry for the way I treated you, okay?"

Percy's ears were met with silence.

"Hello, Kate?"

I had the right to remain silent. I wanted to take in his words, detect signs of sincerity in his voice. I wasn't about to take him back, just like that.

"Hellllooo?"

"Yes, I'm here."

"I said I'm sorry. . . . I'm really, really sorry for the way I treated you. . . . I lost my temper, and I'm sorry about that, okay, sweetheart?"

Percy's shaky voice softened my resolve like Silly Putty. He was sounding so pitiful and sorry right now that I had no other choice but to lower my defenses.

"I accept your apology," I finally said. "It's over and done with."

"So, can I see you today?"

I paused in thought. It was a quiet day. Nothing to do. What the heck. "Yes, I'm free."

"Cool," exclaimed Percy. "I have a special day planned for us. So wear something really nice for me. Okay, sweetheart?"

"Okay, I will," I said. Meanwhile I was thinking, Oh boy, here we go again. What to wear? What to wear?

"I can't wait to see you, baby," said Percy.

For some reason, I didn't respond. I just got the meet-up details, hung up the phone, and immediately started fretting over what to throw over my body.

As soon as I tucked my phone away in its hiding place, it vibrated. I opened the cabinet door back up, pulled out my celly, only to discover a text from Felicia, which raised my blood pressure.

JUST WANT TO LET U KNOW, IT'S NOT OK FOR PERCY TO BE QUESTIONING U LIKE THAT.

HE WASN'T QUESTIONING ME. WE WORKED IT OUT. NO NEED TO WORRY.

IT'S TOO LATE. I'M WORRIED.

WELL, DON'T BE. TTYL.

What a knucklehead, I thought, putting my phone away. If I wasn't so concerned with preparing for my date, I would've called Felicia up to set her completely straight. I wanted to tell her that she had no right to talk down to me like I had no sense when it comes to men. Okay, I really don't have much sense when it comes to them, but she didn't have to be so freaking condescending about it! Who uses phrases like, "It's not ok," to their homegirls? Come on now, let's be for real.

Two seconds later, Felicia actually called me. I sent her butt straight to voice mail. Anyway, back to my date with Percy. I needed something to wear.

Of course *now* I couldn't turn to Felicia for help. So Jeselle ended up saving my day. She hooked me up by letting me borrow her large orange cotton V-neck shirt that was so long it could pass for a cute mini-dress, and her thick brown leather belt adorned my waist. Wasn't the best outfit, but my curvy shape brought the sexy back.

Jeselle flat-ironed my hair, however; it was too thick to get straight, so I wrapped her tan paisley silk scarf around my head, like a headband, and left the back of my hair flowing; I was Afro-puffing it like Foxy Kate, ya dig? Done with that, I slid my black open-toe sandals on my feet, and I was ready to bounce.

"Looking fly, ma," exclaimed Jeselle. "Just get your lip gloss poppin', and you're good to go!"

"Man, listen, you really came through for me," I said.

Jeselle flashed a cheesy grin. "Who got your back, homie?"

"You do." I smiled and reached out to hug her for the first time. Fortunately, Jeselle wasn't afraid to hug, like I used to be. And she had no idea how much our new friendship meant to me.

Because at the moment, it felt like I was about to lose my *best* friend over a silly situation. Of all things, a guy? I didn't want that to happen for nothing in the world. I just needed Felicia to mind her own business; I never stuck my nose in her and Marlon's affairs.

"Why you suddenly look so sad?" asked Jeselle, bringing me back to the present. "Flippin' moods like a light switch."

"Oh . . . it's nothing," I replied, turning away from her concerned stare. "Anyway, my man is waiting. Gotta run."

"Alright, ma, have fun!"

Yeah, I really hoped so. No complications with Percy this time around. No drama. No misunderstandings. This girl just wanted to have fun.

Chapter 19

Percy picked me up on Jay Street at seven o'clock sharp as planned. Before I hopped inside the car, I spotted a single red rose sitting on my seat. "Aw, thank you," I said, sticking my nose inside of the petals to get a good whiff. "Smells really good."

"You're welcome, love."

We drove to Brooklyn Heights, the ritzy part of Brooklyn. When I got out of the car, Percy looked me up and down. "Oh snap, you look like a pumpkin all dressed in orange" he said, chuckling, "but at least your hair looks decent this time."

His words were a lethal blow to my head. Shot down again. I had tried so hard to look good . . . I guessed orange wasn't my color. I just couldn't seem to measure up for him.

On the other hand, Percy looked utterly gorgeous. He wore a button-down crispy white shirt, baggy jeans hanging slightly off his sexy behind. The waves in his hair rippled wonderfully and his edge up was flawless. He was the picture of perfection. Wished he felt the same way about me.

"Let's go," said Percy, grabbing my hand. He led me to an extravagant restaurant situated on the corner of Montague Street. As soon as we stepped inside, a tall, blond hostess rushed up to us. "Table for two?"

She pulled back a red velvet curtain and led us into a plush fancy room full of dressed-up people. When we were seated in a quiet corner, I looked around admiringly at a large mural of Italy on the left wall; the rest of the place was all cream and gold. The tablecloth was cream, the silverware was actually gold. I felt like a queen for the day.

"Classy, right?" said Percy.

"Very," I replied, still looking around in awe. This was the fanciest restaurant I'd ever been in. Percy was right. McDonald's just couldn't compare.

The hostess handed us our menus. There was so much fancy food to choose from. Five minutes later a pretty, slim, light-skinned waitress wearing all black came up to our table. "My name is Bianca, I'll be your server for today."

"Pretty name," said Percy, flashing the same sexy smile he usually flashed me.

Um . . . okay. . . . Well, Bianca was very pretty, and Percy wasn't blind. No need to trip over this . . . I guessed.

"What can I start you off with?" she asked.

I was about to ask Bianca if the chicken Parmesan came with—

"Two glasses of water and the lasagna special, please," Percy, ordered before I could even open my mouth.

I placed the menu down, feeling like a mute fool.

Bianca took our menus and sashayed away. Percy looked after her, but I tried not to let it bother me. I felt so insecure, but I didn't want it showing up in my attitude. So I blurted any old thing to take my mind off the incident. "I've never seen a ceiling painted gold," I said, looking upward.

Percy grabbed my hands and held them for a long time. "Like I told you before, I can show you a whole lot of things. . . . I want to make you happy."

But I didn't feel so happy at the moment.

Out of the blue, Percy started snapping his fingers, rocking in his seat and singing, "I just love to be around you, oh baby. You been so good to me . . ."

"Lenny Williams," I interrupted, trying to stay upbeat. "I like that song, too."

Percy's eyes widened in surprise. "What you know about Lenny Williams, young' un?"

"My foster father used to play his old-school records 24/7," I explained, now smiling at the memory of Ted dancing around the house trying to imitate Lenny. "Oh, oh, oh, oh, I love you," he would croon to Lynn, sounding off-key but extremely sweet.

In all of the houses I had ever lived in, it was rare for me to see a husband crazy about his wife. Singing love songs to her. Showing her respect all day, every day. For instance, this past May, driving downtown with Ted to pick out a gift for Lynn on "Foster" Mother's Day. We were in Macy's, standing on a dumb long line, when a tall brown-skinned woman with ridiculous beauty and curves spun around to ask if she could step out of line real quick. She held up a red silk nightgown and pointed out the unwinding thread at the bottom of it. "No good," she explained.

"No problem, dear," replied Ted, wearing a friendly grin.

The woman must have been encouraged by the word "dear," so when she got back in line, she started forcing small talk on us, batting her eyelashes and smiling the whole time. True, Ted's probably handsome for his age, but dang, have some pride, lady! She was acting so thirsty, I was embarrassed for her. Ted called everybody "dear," even his male boss, just as a running joke.

But the woman pressed on, not catching the hint. "Is that your daughter?" she asked, flashing me a fake smile.

"Sure is," said Ted, without hesitation, making me feel good inside. I felt even better when Ted showed the lady no love, even when she found out he was a mechanic and asked for his business card, clearly trying to get his digits on the slick.

Click.

Ted hung up on her request by simply saying, "Sorry, I ran out of cards." Then he told the thirsty broad to have a nice day. When we left the store, I jokingly said, "Wow, Lynn has you trained!"

"No," he corrected. "Lynn has my heart."

"Okay, player," I said, patting him on the back. "That was a smooth line you just laid on me."

"It's not a line," said Ted, his face turning serious. "It's the truth. And when you're old enough to date, make sure you command the same respect from your guy. Make sure you have his whole heart. Never settle for less."

Never settle for less.

Was I settling for less now? I wondered. I wished Percy would hold me down like Ted did for Lynn. Then again, maybe Ted's discipline came with his age.

But that thought didn't hold weight for long. What about Marlon, even younger than Percy, and holding Felicia down all day, every day? His eyes never strayed to the next chick as far as I could see. As a matter of fact, Marlon was the *first* guy ever to pay my big boobies no mind when I first met him; he kept his pupils trained on Felicia the whole entire time.

"I'm glad you came out with me, baby," said Percy, breaking into my thoughts.

"Me, too," I muttered.

"What's wrong?"

"Nothing," I said, looking down at my lap. Percy reached for my hand across the table and stroked it. "Baby, what's wrong?"

"Nothing," I repeated, forcing a bogus smile. "I'm good," I added.

To make my words match my mood, I tried to think of the bright side. I looked around the elegant restaurant that Percy was nice enough to take me to. This was more than any guy had ever done for me. Might as well be grateful and make the best of my night.

Our food came, smoking off the plate. I was about to dig in, but Percy grabbed the white cloth napkin from the table and told me to put it on my lap. "Oops, my bad," I said, trying to play it off like I knew. If I wasn't mistaken, Percy even shook his head at me.

Well, I wasn't about to embarrass him anymore tonight, so as hungry as I was, I took small, dainty bites of the lasagna. It was delicious, but still, small, dainty bites . . . while Percy wolfed down his food.

Bianca came back to our table. "Is everything okay?" she asked Percy.

"Everything is fine," said Percy. When he said "fine" he emphasized the word, as if he was referring to her. And when Bianca placed the check on our table, she flashed Percy one last googly-eyed smile, and said good-bye to him, barely acknowledging me.

Percy paid. We got up and headed for the exit. I spotted Bianca standing in the corner of the room. Before leaving, I flashed her my famous eye roll, and then sashayed behind Percy, holding my head high.

Once outside, Percy turned to me and said, "Let's take a walk to the Promenade. Ever been there before?"

"No."

"See?" began Percy, "there's always a first time when you're with me."

As we walked down a quiet, cobblestone, tree-lined street, Percy asked, "So did you really enjoy dinner, or were you just gassing my head up?"

"No, it was really good," I said. "Wish I could make lasagna."

"I know how to make lasagna. It's easy."

"You can cook?" I asked, incredulous. I never met a guy who admitted being able to cook. I was impressed.

"Please . . . my mother had me in the kitchen as soon as I was tall enough to reach the stove." Percy's face darkened when he said this.

"Oh," I said, feeling awkward. His mother, again. At least this time, he quickly recovered, thank goodness. And if he could recover so quickly, so could I. I pushed Bianca way in the back of my mind. Maybe I was being too sensitive anyway.

"Matter of fact, I can teach you how to make lasagna," said Percy.

"Wow, really?" I had always wanted to play house with a guy I really liked: him cooking beside me, me washing dishes, him drying. I had all of these romantic scenes in my head and they were finally about to play out with Percy.

We sat on a bench facing the inky-black water, watching the small boats and big ships sail by. The Brooklyn Bridge loomed in the distance. The night summer breeze felt good on my skin. I was feeling so warm and fuzzy in the company of my man. Percy kept grabbing my hand and kissing it, telling me how much he was enjoying himself. I was in seventh heaven. I didn't want the night to end. But as always . . . here comes the curfew countdown.

"Well, I have to go," I said reluctantly.

Percy sighed, got up, and we walked to his car.

Once inside the car, Percy immediately went for my lips. We were parked on a quiet street, so no one was around to see us getting down. Percy was going hard, feeling me up all over, and making me feel so good, like he was yearning for me.

Then he stopped his lips short and told me to climb in the backseat. As I climbed, he reached out and tapped my behind. "Man, baby, you got it going *on*."

Percy settled in beside me and we started going at it hot and heavy again. But when he started sucking ferociously on my neck, as good as it felt, I told him to stop.

"Why?" he asked, panting heavily.

"I don't want a hickey," I said, pushing his lips away.

Percy jerked his head back. "Black as you are?" he exclaimed. "Nobody's going to see it." He busted into chuckles, but then he noticed I wasn't even cracking a smile.

"Honey, what's wrong?" he asked. "You can't take a joke?"

I didn't say anything. I didn't want to argue. I just looked away from Percy and stared out the window deep in thought.

For as long as I could remember, I had a complex about my dark skin, about not being model thin. "You're pretty for a dark-skinned girl" was all I heard growing up. And just when I started saying to myself, "Bump the color-conscious clowns, I'm black and I'm beautiful," now I had my doubts again.

Percy grabbed the bottom of my chin. "Why won't you look at me?"

I had nothing to say.

"So you're going to stay mad at me?"

"I'm not mad," I lied.

When I wouldn't budge on my brooding, Percy huffed, and climbed into the driver's seat. I stayed seated in the back. So he drove me home like a cab driver. And when he tried to kiss me good-bye, I gave him my cheek instead of my lips. I left my rose inside his car on purpose.

YOU LEFT YOUR ROSE.

SORRY. I FORGOT IT.

SO IT DIDN'T MEAN ANYTHING TO YOU?

LIKE I SAID, I FORGOT IT. SAVE IT FOR ME.

IT'S ALREADY DEAD.

Chapter 20

Percy didn't contact me for three days. I didn't bother reaching out to him, either. I was still upset, and it's never good to communicate when you're upset. I wasn't so sure if Percy's words were reason enough to *end* our relationship, but I knew I was surely hurt by them.

As disappointed as I was, I had to admit: I missed Percy. Three whole days without him had dragged by like a year. I had gotten so used to Percy's daily texts, checking up on his "baby." I had gotten so used to Percy period, the first real boyfriend in my life.

So when Percy texted me three days later, I can't even front, the butterflies revived inside my stomach; and his foul "hickey" comment flew right out the window like an annoying fly swatted far away from my mind.

Percy asked me if I could come over to his father's apartment to learn how to make lasagna. Of course, I could, was my reply. So Percy ran down the meet-up plan. And I flew out the house anxious to see my man.

I was picked up at the Jay Street station. Percy passionately kissed me hello like we hadn't seen each other in years. His usual intensity overpowered me so much, I leaned my head back in exhaustion after the kiss.

We drove to Pathmark to buy the lasagna ingredients. On the

way, Trey Songz singing "You Belong to Me," was pumping through the speakers, and Percy kept reaching over to caress my hand, while he steered his wheel with the other.

I felt so loved and adored.

When we stepped inside the brightly lit supermarket, my ecstatic feelings continued. We walked up and down the aisle searching for ingredients, giggling with each other, comparing prices; it felt like we were an old married couple. Shucks, I even pictured a baby girl riding inside of our shopping cart. I noticed women shooting wistful glances at us. I couldn't blame them. We looked mad cute together.

Percy paid for everything, and kissed me on the cheek in front of the cashier. I felt so special. I can't even begin to explain how special I felt.

We hopped back inside the car. Then Percy drove to DUMBO at breakneck speed. My heart was in my throat the whole time.

As soon as we walked inside Percy's father's apartment, he set down the bags and pressed me against the hallway wall. He tongued me down for ten minutes straight. His feverish need for me was so incredible. The way he held me in his arms so tightly, like he never wanted to let me go. I swear, it felt like any minute, he could get *it*. We shared so much earth-shaking passion between us; our chemistry was off the Richter scale. It was taking all of my might not to give in.

"Okay, baby," said Percy, pulling himself together. "Let's get it popping in the kitchen."

"No doubt," I replied, all giggly. "Show me the oven!"

First, Percy handed me a knife, an onion, and instructed me on how to chop it into shreds. My eyes were burning and watering like mad, so I said, "Cutting onions is not a game!"

"Yeah, that's why I have you doing it." Percy laughed.

"Aww, that's not right," I joked. "Why do *I* have to do all the dirty work?"

"Because you're the woman of the house," said Percy, smiling. "That's what you're supposed to do."

I chuckled slightly, but my eyes were not amused. I wiped a tear away.

Finally, I got through with the tortuous onions. Then Percy poured the chopped onions and ground beef into a pan. He boiled a box of noodles and when they were done, he showed me how to peel them off of each other by running cold water over them.

Everything was coming along nicely. The meat was simmering and smelling good. My stomach growled.

"Sounds like you got a rabid dog inside your tummy," said Percy.

"I know, right?" I giggled.

Percy stood behind me as I followed his instructions, adding layers on top of layers of ricotta and mozzarella cheese. I was having so much fun.

Done with my duty, Percy grinned at me and said, "I see you're a pro at this."

"Oh, yes, I am." I laughed and hugged him, feeling myself opening up to him even more. "Thanks for teaching me."

"You're welcome, Baby." Percy kissed me, and then patted my behind.

The lasagna was lip-smacking delicious. I wanted seconds, but the other day Percy had made a comment about my weight. So I wasn't about to reload my plate.

After we washed and dried the dishes, we lounged arm and arm on the couch.

"That was so good," I said, "I can't believe I just made lasagna." I leaned my head against Percy's chest.

"*We* just made lasagna," corrected Percy. "We're a team, remember?"

"True," I said. "And now that I can actually cook, I'll be one step ahead when I get to Green Hills."

"What's Green Hills?" he asked.

I explained the whole independent-living program and Percy looked so sad after I gave him the explanation.

He softly caressed my face and said, "Kate, if *we* work out, you won't have to be moving to another facility. We could get our own place together."

I thought Percy was joking, so I smirked.

"Wipe that silly look off your face. I'm serious. What? You don't see us being together?"

"I do . . . but—"

"But what?" Percy interjected. "Don't you know how much I love you?"

I just stared at him, dumbfounded.

"I love you," repeated Percy, looking deeply into my eyes. This was my first time ever hearing these three words from a guy on the serious tip. I felt overwhelmed. Too overwhelmed to say the words back.

"Don't you love me?" asked Percy.

I nodded, feeling rushed off my feet.

"I don't read sign language, sweetheart. Do you love me?"

"Yes."

"Then tell me you love me."

"I love you."

Boom. I said it. Now it was official.

Percy caressed my face. "I'm giving you all that I have . . . so please don't play me." His eyes were blazing with full concentration on me.

"I won't play you," I said. He squeezed my hand tightly, and stared at me deeply.

Percy's intensity was almost ruining this beautiful moment.

"Kate, I don't think you understand how much I care about you," Percy pressed on.

"I do understand."

"Then act like you know, sweetheart. Don't look so afraid about what I'm saying to you."

Percy grabbed my chin and brought my face close to his. First, he he kissed me gently on my mouth, suckled my bottom lip, and then he kissed with so much force and passion, I melted into him. My body drifted away from my mind. I was burning inside. I matched his tongue movements stroke for stroke, even threw my arms around his neck and held on to him mad tight.

"So, when can I make love to you?" Percy whispered in my ear.

My arms dropped away from his neck. Here we go again.

"I don't know . . . soon," I said.

"How soon?"

Obviously, he wasn't going to stop questioning me about it, so I had to think of a bulletproof excuse. "Percy . . . trust me . . . I want you, too . . . but you already know it's illegal for us to have sex . . . because of our age difference—"

"And?" he interrupted.

"And I don't want you going to jail over me."

Percy jerked his head back. "You plan on telling somebody?"

"No."

"Okay, then, what are you saying?"

"Percy . . . please don't take this personal. . . . I'm just not ready. . . . It has nothing to do with you."

"Listen, just forget it," he snapped.

And just like before, Percy looked mad disappointed. Without a word, he got up and went into the bedroom. He stayed in there for a while. And then he took a trip to the bathroom. Then he went into the kitchen, walking around aimlessly, opening cabinets and closing them with a bang.

He had left me on the couch, sitting there like, duh? What just happened? But I wasn't about to follow him around like a lost little puppy. I knew in my heart I was in the right. He was in the wrong. *Real* love waits for sex, point-blank period.

I sat in my spot self-righteously until Percy returned to me. When he finally came back, he clicked on the television, and pulled me up into his lap, like nothing had happened.

I blinked. A brand-new Percy. Just like that.

He started massaging my back. Then he reached down and removed my sandals and began rubbing my stubby unpolished toes; even more confirmation that he had to love me. I'm saying, who does that?

"Feels nice," I said, in ecstasy.

"I can make you feel even better . . . if you let me."

Just then, my phone rang in my pocket. I was about to ignore the call, but Percy told me to answer it. Before answering, I was about to get up from Percy's lap, but he pulled me back down. So I answered from where I sat.

"Hey, Kate . . . I need to talk to you," blurted Felicia.

"Who's that?" Percy asked.

I was hoping Felicia didn't hear Percy. Apparently, she did because she said, "Oh, you're with *him* now."

"Yeah," I said. Then I took the phone away from my mouth and whispered to Percy, "It's Felicia."

"Tell her you're with your man right now."

When I got back on the phone, I told Felicia I had to go.

"Oh," she said. I could tell she was holding back words.

Click.

Just in case she tried to call me again, I secretly pushed the "off" button on my Pearl; I had to do it slick. Didn't want Percy getting suspicious over why I had to turn off my phone.

After that fiasco, nine o'clock rolled around. I told Percy I had to go.

"Damn, Kate, I really wish you could stay with me all night."

"Me, too," I said.

"I mean, we don't have to have sex. I just want to hold you in my arms all night."

"Yeah, that would be nice."

"So then, let's make it happen."

"Okay, I'll try."

"You'll try?" asked Percy. "That doesn't sound so convincing."

"Okay, I will," I stated firmly. I didn't want to upset Percy again.

"When?"

"Soon," I said, vaguely. "I promise . . . real soon."

Luckily, I really had to go, so he didn't press me further.

Chapter 21

Bright and early in the morning, Belinda called for me from downstairs. "You have a visitor," she announced.

Oh really? I thought. Who could it be? I knew Percy wouldn't risk getting me into trouble. I was mystified. When I got downstairs, Belinda nodded her head toward the door, which was cracked halfway open. I hesitantly made my way to the threshold, and *boom*, there was Felicia, standing on the porch, looking nervous and fidgety. She wore a bright yellow T-shirt, black yoga pants, her favorite busted yellow sneakers, and she was holding a manila envelope close to her chest.

"Sorry I came unannounced," she began, "but you refuse to return my calls."

I paused, still taken aback by her presence. "Um, I been real busy," I finally managed to say, feeling bad for dodging my best friend all this time.

"Well, I just came to give you this," she said, handing me the envelope. "My mother is parked a few cars down. So I can't stay long."

Dang, she even had her mother bring her here? I scanned the street and sure enough, three cars down, I spotted Felicia's mother sitting in their shiny black SL550 Benz.

"What is this about?" I asked, apprehensively staring at the envelope.

"You'll see," said Felicia. "Just don't open it until I leave, please."

My goofy, loveable homegirl was now acting so cold and businesslike toward me; it was hard to take.

"Well, alrighty then," I began, slowly. "So, um, can I call you later?"

"Of course you can," said Felicia. "That's why I'm here. I need to talk to you."

"Okay, but really . . . I meant to call you back. . . . I just been mad busy."

"Okay, Kate," said Felicia. "Whatever you say."

Felicia's mother tapped the horn twice. Felicia's cue to go. Good, because I felt the tension thickening in the air between us.

Felicia gave me a stiff hug good-bye and reminded me to call her.

"I will," I promised.

But once I was locked safely inside the bathroom, and ripped open the envelope, I wasn't sure *when* I'd be calling that fool.

I sat on the tub's edge, and muttered, "Is she serious right now?" as I laid eyes on an Abuse Facts Sheet, five pages long. I couldn't believe Felicia had really taken it there. But like a car wreck you can't look away from, my eyes gravitated toward some of the warning signs, including: frequent check-ins on a mate's whereabouts, bursts of bad temper, name calling and put-downs, controlling the way one dresses, eats, talks. . . . I couldn't read any further. None of these warning signs *really* applied to Percy. But then again . . .

I blocked the words out my head. I ripped the sheets to shreds, balled up the scraps, and made a three-point shot into the bathroom's garbage can.

Relationships can be so confusing. When you're in a shaky situation your mind starts leaving out the bad parts of your guy, and concentrates on the good, painting pretty little pictures in your head. I know there's a bad side to Percy, but the good in him outweighs the bad. I feel happy and loved whenever I'm around Percy. Never in my life have I felt this way before. I want to be happy, just like Felicia is with Marlon. Nobody's perfect. Everybody gets mad in their own way. Too bad Felicia doesn't understand. It's best to avoid her right now. She has too many questions I have no answers for.

Chapter 22

Five o'clock on a Saturday morning, Jeselle rapped hard on our window. I was the first to wake up, groggy as ever, and pulled the window open for her. She struggled over the sill to get her long limbs inside. Even in the darkness of the room, I could see her eyes were watery.

"What's wrong?" I asked, still half-dazed, but alert enough to be concerned.

"My mother has a new boyfriend. She kicked me out. Can't visit her anymore . . . ever."

"Wow."

"Yeah, it's a wrap." Jeselle sniffed.

"Let's go in the bathroom to talk," I suggested. I didn't want to wake up Tracy. I didn't want her in the conversation. This was a delicate matter.

I turned on the bathroom's nightlight instead of the bright light, and Jeselle and I sat on the edge of the tub next to each other. It was so hurtful to see big and bad Jeselle reduced to a puddle of tears.

I scooted closer to her and wrapped my arm around her shoulder. "Keep your head up, ma. It's going to be okay." I repeated this over and over again.

Keeping my head up was the only way I knew how to cope with

my own parentless condition. Shucks, at least Jeselle's mother had tried and failed instead of not trying at all. My own parents abandoned me before I could even walk.

And if you ask me, Jeselle was better off without a mother who fought her like a stranger in the street. Just because a woman has a child doesn't make her a real mother.

However, Jeselle *didn't* ask me for my opinion, so I didn't dare offer one. Folks get mighty touchy when you jump on their loved ones, even if their loved ones are already jumping on them.

"You good?" I asked, before leaving the bathroom.

"Yeah, I'm okay," Jeselle finally said.

But later that day, she moped around the house and all of the girls were asking her what was wrong. To take Jeselle's mind off of things, I asked if she wanted to cash in on an earlier promise to cornbraid her hair. "Yeah, that's cool," she said. "But I don't want to be in this house. Let's go out on the back porch. I need some air."

"No problem," I said. The backyard wasn't so bad now that Gerald's lazy butt had finally cut the grass. The only downside was that we had a clearer view of the cemetery.

I grabbed my comb and brush, Jeselle grabbed a folding chair, and we carried ourselves out to the back porch. I didn't expect to see the rest of the crew already outside passing a fat blunt around. Two were sitting on the railing, and three on the steps. I placed the chair six feet away from them, trying to avoid the smoke.

As soon as Jeselle sat down, Tracy got up, passed Jeselle the blunt, and said, "Burn it down, chick."

Jeselle took her puff and passed it up to me. "Nah, I'm good," I said.

"You square as hell." Jeselle laughed.

Instead of taking offense, I joked back, "You don't want me braiding your hair while I'm high, do you?"

Jeselle chuckled at this. I even thought I heard Tracy chuckle, too.

Then I got to work on Jeselle's hair. This was my first time working with such long hair; it wasn't as easy as I thought. But I was determined to hook her up, especially with her feeling so down and all. I parted her hair carefully, and concentrated all my efforts to tighten every braid.

The girls were busy getting nice with their weed, so they weren't loud and distracting me, thank goodness.

In the middle of braiding, I had to stop to use the bathroom. While in there, I pulled my phone out from the cleaning cabinet to check for messages.

I had a missed call from Felicia. Ignored that. And then there was Percy's text:

CALL ME AS SOON AS YOU GET THIS.

CAN I CALL YOU LATER?

I NEED TO SPEAK WITH YOU RIGHT NOW.

Normally, I tried not to make phone calls in the bathroom. I didn't want the girls thinking I was crazy and talking to myself. But since Percy said "right now," I called him immediately.

"Baby, why are you whispering?" he asked.

"I'm in the bathroom," I explained. "Can't talk loud."

"What you doing right now? Can I see you?"

I paused, thinking of Jeselle's half-done head and her jacked-up spirits. Nah, I couldn't leave my girl hanging like that. "Um . . . is tomorrow okay?"

"But I want to see you today."

"My friend needs me right now."

"What friend?"

"Jeselle."

"But what does Jeselle have over me?"

"Nothing," I said, exasperated. "I'm just doing her hair."

"You're always doing somebody's hair," Percy complained.

Now that was a boldfaced lie, but I didn't bother to address it.

"Please, baby? I want to see you. I really miss you," pleaded Percy.

I almost gave in to him, but the image of Jeselle's watery eyes caught my soul. "I'm sorry, my friend needs me."

"But *I* need you," said Percy.

"She's going through something," I tried to explain. And it was none of Percy's business what Jeselle was going through, so I finally grew some guts, lied, and said someone was knocking on the door. I had to go.

Percy hung up on me without even saying good-bye.

I went back outside, walked through the cloud of blunt smoke, and asked Jeselle to hand me the comb. My mood was mighty low.

"Dang, what took you so long?" asked Jeselle. "I thought you got flushed down the toilet." The girls busted out laughing. I chuckled, wanting to be a good sport.

"You okay?" asked Jeselle.

"Yeah, I'm good," I lied, and resumed working on Jeselle's head. My braids were coming out dumb fly. Ciara thought so, too. She stood over Jeselle's head and said, "You do hair better than those African braiders."

I looked up into her eyes that were bloodshot from weed. "Thanks," I said, shaking Percy out of my mind.

Then Tracy rolled up behind Jeselle's head and said, "Your parting skills are mad precise." The friendly tone in her voice surprised the heck out of me.

"Thanks," I said, flashing a grin. It was such a relief to finally be cool with my roommate—not best buddies—but at least cool.

Venus rushed up to me and asked, "Can you do me next?"

"Yeah, no problem."

"How much you charging?" she asked.

"It's okay, I got you," I said. "They barely give us pocket change up in here, so I don't expect you to pay me."

Venus clapped her hands twice and said, "Chick, please, I can afford it. I don't depend on no allowance. That's what boyfriends are for."

Well, I wasn't about to beg her *not* to pay me, so I said, "Okay, thirty dollars." I needed the money anyway.

I braided the last braid in Jeselle's hair, and stood back to admire my work. As soon as Jeselle got up to go check her hair, Venus bum rushed the seat, yelling, "I got next!"

Then Jeselle came back outside smiling from ear to ear. She hugged me mad tight, and said, "You just hooked a sister up!"

"You know I got you, homie," I replied, reaching up to smooth down the top of her fresh long braids.

"So every week you got me?" Jeselle joked.

"Shoot, if I had bomb hair like yours, I'd never put it in braids. My hair would be flowing with the wind all day, every day."

"Whatever," Jeselle said, flipping her hand in the air. "People always think they want what they don't have. Shoot, I'm ready to cut my hair bald."

"Are you crazy," I exclaimed. "You better not!"

Venus tapped me and said, "Um, when are you planning on getting started? I'm a paying customer!"

Jeselle laughed. "My bad, let me leave Kate alone. Go 'head and do your thing, ma." She stepped aside.

I started in on Venus's thick head of hair.

Out of the blue, I said to Jeselle, "Percy says he prefers longer hair."

"Oh yeah?" said Jeselle, raising her eyebrows. "Well, tell *Percy* to buy you a damn weave then." She cracked up at her own joke. I chuckled, but for some reason, I suddenly felt sad.

I DON'T UNDERSTAND WHY YOU COULDN'T MAKE TIME FOR ME TODAY.

MY FRIEND NEEDED ME.

BUT I NEEDED YOU. AND I'M MORE THAN YOUR FRIEND. I'M SUPPOSED TO BE YOUR MAN.

I KNOW.

CAN I SEE YOU TOMORROW?

YES, I CAN SEE YOU.

MEET ME AT JAY STREET. THREE O'CLOCK. MAYBE WE CAN GO TO PROSPECT PARK.

SOUNDS GOOD.

CALL ME LATER TONIGHT. I WANT TO HEAR YOUR VOICE BEFORE I GO TO SLEEP.

OK.

I called Percy at eleven o'clock that night. Nobody was downstairs guarding the phone, so I had taken a chance with the landline. When Percy answered, he sounded so happy to hear from me. He asked me how I was feeling. I told him I was fine. He said he was fine, too. Our conversation was going along just fine until he broke the spell by asking, "So what was wrong with your homegirl?"

Here we go again.

I had already promised myself that Jeselle's business was none of his, but Percy wasn't the type to leave things alone. He always pressed and pressed until he got the answers he felt he deserved. Well, I was not in the mood to be pressed tonight, so I gave him a snippet of what happened, and ended with, "Jeselle got slapped by her own mother in front of this new loser boyfriend."

"Oh man, Jeselle is crying over a little slap?" asked Percy in disbelief. "Please, that's nothing. My mother broke a broomstick over my head once just for spilling Kool-Aid on the carpet."

"Your mother beat you with a broomstick?" I stuttered in shock. I knew Mrs. Thomas was a witch, but I didn't think she was a *violent* one.

"Broomsticks, belts, extension cords . . . whatever she could grab."

Wow, I said to myself, shaking my head in disgust. My heart went out to Percy. I mean, I had been beaten by many foster parents before, but never by my own flesh and blood—wherever they might be.

Percy suddenly added, “Don’t get it twisted, sweetheart; you said ‘beats’ as in present tense. I’m talking about back when I was young. My mother knows better than to try that mess with me now.”

Awkward silence fell over the phone.

Then I heard footsteps creaking on the stairs.

“Someone’s coming,” I whispered. “I gotta go.”

“I’m looking forward to tomorrow, sweetheart,” said Percy. “I can’t wait to hold you in my arms again.”

Chapter 23

First thing in the morning, I peered out of my bedroom window. Storm clouds wrapped a huge gray blanket over Brooklyn. Oh well, I thought, Prospect Park was clearly out. This was a day to be inside with your boo. Sure enough, my boo was thinking the same thing, too. I received his text at twelve o'clock on the dot.

WEATHER SUCKS, BUT I STILL WANT TO SEE YOU.
SAME HERE.
CHINESE FOOD AND A MOVIE?
SOUNDS GREAT.

I met Percy at Jay Street at three o'clock. Then he drove us to a giant video store. We stepped inside the joint holding hands like an adorable couple. I witnessed lonesome people staring blankly at the huge movie selection, and sassy couples bickering about which movie to pick.

I didn't go through the trouble of bickering with Percy about movies. I just let my man take control; I doubted he would let me do the picking anyway.

In less than ten minutes, Percy snatched up two new releases. I didn't bother to look, or ask, for the titles. What mattered most to me was the upcoming opportunity to be snuggled up on the couch with my baby. Oh yeah.

We stood on a long line waiting to check out our movies, still holding hands, Percy bending down to kiss me on the cheek every few minutes. When our turn finally came, we were served by a tall, bucktoothed cashier. He greeted us in a loud, lively voice. "Great day for a movie, isn't it?"

Since Percy didn't say anything, I piped in, "For sure."

The cashier held up one of our movies and said, "I don't want to ruin it for you, but the butler did it."

The cashier was so corny, but he was older, and reminded me of Ted with his dry jokes, so I was chuckling at everything he said.

I didn't realize that Percy had a problem with this, until we got inside his car. Before he cranked the engine, he turned to me and said, "So you like attention, huh?"

"What?" I asked, jerking my head back in confusion.

"Why were you flirting with that guy so hard?"

"What guy?" I asked, because he surely couldn't be referring to the doofy cashier. If I'm going to flirt with someone, *at least* he's going to be a dime. Doofy dude was a penny; I wasn't attracted to his old butt at all.

"So you think it's cute to disrespect me out in public?" demanded Percy.

I was truly stunned by this accusation. All I could do was sit in silence as Percy yelled at me, asking the same stupid question over and over again.

"I wasn't flirting," I said, hopefully for the last time.

"Yes, you were."

"No, I wasn't."

"Yes, you were!"

I turned from him to stare out the window, disappointed and confused.

"I don't know why you feel the need to lie to me," said Percy. "I was standing right there. I saw you flirting with him!"

Okay, I had enough. I didn't have to put up with this bull, especially because I was completely innocent. "Listen, if you're not going to believe me, can you please take me to the train station? I want to go home." Now I was close to tears.

"I'm not going anywhere until you answer my question."

"If you can't take me, then I'm leaving." I grabbed the car door handle as a threat. I had never seen Percy this angry before. He was starting to scare me.

"You're leaving me because you're guilty," spat Percy, his light brown eyes blazing with anger.

I yanked the door open, got out, and slammed it shut behind me. Percy yelled out his car window, "Don't be slamming my doors, stupid!"

"You're the one who's stupid," I yelled back, surprised that I was actually cracking back on him. I had been holding in a whole lot since being with Percy.

I started walking down the block, my head bent down low, bewilderment coursing through my brain. Did that really just happen? Out of nowhere? Wow.

The fiery red Avenger trailed me, its crazy owner still shouting at me. "If you need attention that bad, you don't need to be with a guy like me. My woman has to show me respect. You hear me? Respect!"

I just couldn't wrap my mind around the sudden turn of events. This couldn't be the same guy who had done so many sweet and thoughtful things for me.

I didn't recognize Percy anymore.

Just then, I felt a raindrop fall on my eyelid. How appropriate, because I was already starting to cry. This was supposed to be a nice, simple day: Chinese food, a movie, and me and my man cuddled on the couch. But now, I was about to get stormed on. I needed my umbrella, which was still inside Percy's car. Damn.

Percy still had his head stuck out the window, shouting out craziness and trailing me, so I asked in the nicest tone possible, "Can I just get my umbrella please?"

He fixed me with a mean stare and yelled "You should have thought about that before you disrespected me."

Beeeppp! Beeeppp! Cars were now honking at Percy who was holding up traffic. So he peeled off down the street, leaving me in the dust . . . or should I say the rain. Lightning lit up the sky, and then came the snap, crackle, and pop. Drops began to fall in sheets, drenching me instantly. I was a wet, cold mess.

I walked with my head down being pummeled by the rain. Six long blocks to go. When I finally made it inside the train station, I was soaking wet and crying.

During my long train ride home, I shivered with cold and hurt over what had just happened. . . . It was supposed to be a nice, simple day.

Later that night, I received a text from Percy:

DID YOU MAKE IT HOME OKAY?

I left his question dangling in the air.

Chapter 24

I'M SORRY FOR GOING OFF ON YOU, BABY. PLEASE DON'T BE MAD AT ME.

I GO CRAZY WHEN I THINK OF YOU BEING WITH SOMEONE ELSE.

KATE, I NEED YOU IN MY LIFE, BABY. PLEASE DON'T DO THIS TO ME.

PLEASE CALL ME, SWEETHEART. I PROMISE IT WON'T HAPPEN AGAIN.

WHY WON'T YOU WRITE ME BACK?

LET ME MAKE IT UP TO YOU, BABY. TEXT ME WHEN YOU GET A CHANCE.

Yeah, fat chance. In less than twenty-four hours, Percy was actually expecting me to give him a clean slate? Hell no! I ignored all of Percy's texts. I was too upset, and like I said, it's never good to communicate when you're upset. I needed a moment. Matter of fact, more than a moment. Making me walk in the pouring rain was something only a cruel person could do. So should I break up with Percy? Or give him another chance? My mind was split in two.

A part of me wanted it to be over, but the other part was holding out hope, remembering the good times, so many good times. I needed to sort this whole thing out in my head.

Problem was, Percy wouldn't give me a chance to clear my brain. He texted me twenty more apologetic messages, no exaggeration, before I finally decided to give in and text him back.

I JUST WISHED YOU BELIEVED ME. THAT'S ALL.

I DO BELIEVE YOU NOW.

AND I PROMISE NOT TO GO OFF ON YOU LIKE THAT AGAIN, OK, BABY?

OK.

Now don't get me wrong. My "OK" meant, yes, I hear you, now please fall back from texting me, and give me some freaking space.

But Percy texted me ten more times, begging me back into his life.

Lucky for me, I had gotten sick from being drenched in the rain, so it was easy for me to put down my phone and stay away from Percy. I was glued to my bed for three whole days with the covers pulled up over my head. Chicken soup, hot tea, and Jeselle made me feel better.

When I fully recuperated, and checked my phone, no lie, I had about fifty texts from Percy apologizing fifty different ways.

I went through all of his "sorry" messages, pressing the Delete button, and shaking my head in disbelief. He was so extra. Borderline obnoxious.

Then suddenly, one text caught my attention. It said the following:

AUGUST 4TH OUR ONE-MONTH ANNIVERSARY. I WANT US TO DO SOMETHING SPECIAL. I REALLY MISS U.

First, I was surprised that Percy actually remembered our special day, because I had forgotten it. Second, I started thinking that Percy must really care about me to be so persistent to the point of pitiful. Super fly guys like him are usually not willing to lose their pride, sending a million texts, begging some girl for forgiveness when they have so many other prettier girls to choose from. In all of my years, no boy has ever fought so hard to keep me in his life.

So maybe Percy truly loved me, I told myself. Maybe he was only having a bad day that day, and maybe, just maybe, I *did* disrespect him for being too friendly to the cashier, and maybe we all lose control at times . . . the truth is, nobody's perfect. Besides, as out of control as *I* used to be, who was I to judge Percy? Where would I be if Tisha had given up on me?

With these thoughts running through my brain, I finally caved in and texted Percy back. I told him that I missed him, too, which was so very true. A split second later, Percy popped the question:

CAN YOU COME TO DUMBO AND SPEND THE NIGHT WITH ME TOMORROW?

It didn't take me long to text back: YES.

I missed Percy. Really missed him. I wanted to be wrapped up in his beautiful strong arms again. I couldn't wait to feel his warm sensuous lips against my skin.

Operation DUMBO was about to be in full effect.

As far as the group home was concerned, I wasn't worried about a spend-the-night strategy. By now, everybody at Common Grounds was doing the same overnight thing; so just add a sister to the mix. My only concern was Percy's expectations. He promised that our night didn't have to be about sex if I didn't want it to be. Well, I didn't want it to be. I was determined to hold down my get-to-know-me-first rule. Abstaining from sex was the only power I had over Percy. And I wasn't about to lose my power just yet.

"I need you to take a cab to my father's apartment," Percy explained, when I had snuck a call to him later that night. "Be at the crib by eight o'clock."

Percy gave me his father's exact address. Meanwhile, I was thinking, Who has money for a cab?

Luckily, Percy read my mind and further explained, "Call me when you're close by, and I'll come downstairs to pay."

"Okay."

The plan was tightly set.

Time to pack my bag.

Jeselle sat on my bed watching me fumble through my dresser drawer looking for some overnight gear. "Girl, you better pull out some sexy lingerie," she exclaimed.

"Nah, it's not about sex tonight," I said with a chuckle.

"Homegirl, you better get your mind right and let Percy hit it before he finds somebody else."

Jeselle's words rang in my head like a warning bell.

But then the memory of Tisha's advice bing-bonged even louder: "Kate, don't give up your treasure to just any old body. Make sure the guy is worth it first. If he loves you, he will wait."

Now that's what's up.

With this comforting thought in mind, I threw my overnight bag on the bed, and began packing.

But Jeselle broke into my thoughts again by saying, "If Percy fine as you say, best believe he's getting skins from someone else."

"Well, Percy already told me he can wait," I firmly stated. Jeselle was about to get on my last nerves if she didn't zip it. Loved her, but she really needed to zip it. She didn't know what she was talking about. Besides, girls and guys be jumping between thighs without bothering to get themselves, or their partners, checked. I wanted to take a trip to the clinic with Percy before I gave him my treasure.

Show him I am clean; and let him do the same. Only problem was, I doubted he'd be game.

Anyway.

I purposely packed my big-girl panties and sports bra, figuring no need to be tempting a brother with lacy lingerie. If Percy peeped me in droopy granny panties, he probably wouldn't be wanting me too tough.

Jeselle cracked up hard at the sight of my underwear, though. "Are those curtains?" she asked between guffaws. "Or a pillowcase? Girl, you got some big old drawers!"

"Whatever, I'm all set," I said, grinning, my bag over my shoulder, my feet pointing toward the doorway.

"Well, have fun tonight," said Jeselle, giggling mischievously.

"Don't worry, I will." I smiled, feeling elated. I couldn't wait to be back in my baby's arms again.

Chapter 25

At first, everything was going according to plan. Mrs. Cooper was long gone. Belinda and Gerald, missing in action as usual. At fifteen minutes after seven, I took flight from the group home, thinking my estimated time of arrival to DUMBO would be on point.

But when I hit the streets, I couldn't find a cab for nothing. Avenue U, empty. Stillwell Avenue, plenty of cars but no cabs.

I nervously checked my BlackBerry. There was only one battery bar left. Now I had to turn my phone off to save power. Not a good look, since I wouldn't be able to call Percy and tell him I couldn't catch a cab to save my life.

Gravesend was a ghost town. No exaggeration, I had to walk thirteen blocks before I finally hit a busy intersection. Sadly enough, three cabs passed me by on purpose; I know because they looked dead at me as I waved for them to stop.

Then, finally, a shiny silver cab raced up to the curb like a victorious chariot, ready to save my night. I hopped inside, told the cabby where to go, and he whisked me away.

"Excuse me, sir, what time is it?" I asked, as we cruised down a dark stretch of road.

The cabby needlessly swiveled all the way around and said, "A little after eight o'clock, honey. You late for a date?"

I didn't answer him. I was too busy fretting. I was indeed late. I had tried my best not to disappoint Percy. But it seemed like everything I did led to his disappointment.

When we finally headed down Percy's father's block, I pulled out my phone, which was hanging on to its last bar.

"Yeah?" Percy answered in a monotone voice.

"I'm downstairs."

Click.

The phone went dead. I wasn't sure if we had a bad connection, or did Percy just hang up on me? For some reason, my hands were shaking.

As soon as I caught sight of Percy, I knew he was upset. His body language was stiff and his face mad rigid. He didn't look my way once when he came up to the cab, holding a billfold. "Here you go, my man," he said, peeling off the cab fare. He must have given a nice tip because the cabby exclaimed, "Thanks, and have a wonderful time, lovebirds!"

Well, this bird wanted to fly away because Percy was showing me no love. My heart felt like a stone sinking inside my stomach, as Percy ignored the mess out of me.

He was quiet as I followed him up the stairwell. But as soon as we were behind closed doors, he got up in my face and said, "What took you so long?"

"I had a hard time finding a cab," I stuttered. Percy backed me up close to the wall, and slammed his hand against it. I jerked my shoulders up in shock.

"I told you to get here at eight o'clock," Percy shouted. "You couldn't make a simple phone call to tell me you were running late?"

"I'm sorry," I said. "My battery was running low."

Percy walked away from me, shaking his head. I followed behind him into the living room.

The living room was dark, lit by candles sitting in ceramic holders on each side table. I smelled strawberry incense floating in the air. Percy had tried to set moods, and the mood was now ruined. I plopped down heavily on the couch, and placed my overnight bag beside me to keep me company.

Percy was pacing around the living room, with his hands behind his back. "Couldn't even make a simple phone call," he said, more to himself than me. I cast my eyes down to the carpet to avoid his angry glare.

Then out of nowhere, Percy swooped down and snatched my overnight bag from the couch. He stormed into the nearby kitchen, and flipped on the light. I could see him from the overpass, digging furiously through my bag.

"I gave you this phone to keep in touch with you," Percy shouted. "You're supposed to have it on 24/7." He fumbled through my bag, yanked out my BlackBerry, and said, "So let's see who you been calling."

He had a right to be mad at me, but now he was overdoing it. I didn't say anything, though. I was too scared; he was too angry.

After Percy finished checking my BlackBerry's call log, of course he found nothing.

I thought my proven innocence would calm him down. But I thought dead wrong. The next thing I knew, Percy's arm pitched back like he was playing baseball, and a split second later, the Blackberry came hurtling toward my head. I ducked in the nick of time. The phone just missed the glass coffee table and landed with a thud on the plush beige carpet. I curled up on the couch into a fetal position, shocked as hell and frightened to death.

Percy stormed into the living room and stood over me. "I had everything planned out for us, trying to make our night special, and you messed it all up."

"I'm sorry," I said, shielding my face.

"Put your hand down," he snapped. "I'm not going to hit you."

I unshielded my eyes.

"How could you do this to me, Kate?" he asked, his voice a bit calmer, "Look at everything I tried to do for you."

Percy grabbed my hand, lifted me from the couch, and took me on a tour of ruined romance. First, he led me into the kitchen, lifted the lid of the garbage can, and showed me a glob of uneaten mashed potatoes, corn on the cob, and fried chicken mixed with potato peels. A part of me thought this extreme of him, throwing away good food that could have simply been warmed up. But the other part of me was touched; he had cooked us a delicious dinner for our anniversary, all for nothing.

Then Percy led me inside the bathroom. Two candles sat on either side of the tub. Red and white rose petals were scattered all over the tub's edge and the white tiled floor. The bathroom even smelled like roses. The tub was filled up to the brim, with a few bubbles still floating lifelessly around. A fluffy white towel and a brand-new red robe sat atop the wicker hamper situated in the corner. "I remember you complaining about having no hot water at your house," Percy began, "so I ran a hot bath for you . . . but now look." He dipped his hand in the water. "Ice cold." He flicked the water at me. "I should make you get in it," he added.

I was almost tempted to hop in the cold water just to show him how sorry I was. I mean . . . look at everything he tried to do for me, and all I had to do was simply keep my phone charged. Nobody had ever done anything this special for me. Romance was for people in the movies before I met Percy. My first *real* boyfriend had tried to treat me like a lady, and I had acted like an irresponsible little girl. I looked down at the floor. I felt so bad. "I'm really sorry," I said. "I just wasn't thinking."

Percy must have sensed my sorrow, because he finally calmed all the way down.

"I'm tired," he rasped, in a hoarse voice. "Let's go to bed."

"Baby?"

"Yes?"

"I'm sorry for throwing the phone at you." We lay in the big soft bed, our bodies intertwined like a pretzel.

I didn't know what to say.

If I said, "It's okay," that would make Percy think he could throw phones at me again, but if I told him that it *better not* happen again, that would make us get into an argument. So I said nothing. Absolutely nothing.

"Did you hear me?" asked Percy, rubbing my arm with his warm hands.

"Yes, I heard you."

"And I promise it won't happen again, okay, baby? It's just that I was trying to do something nice for you and you made me upset. Do you forgive me?"

I nodded in the dark.

Percy rubbed my leg. I could tell he was going to try me again. But I was fortified down there. Wide awake, mad alert, determined to keep Percy out of my panties. I brushed his groping hand from the side of my grannies, from the top, front and back. Finally, he gave up the struggle and left me alone. I think he would've pressed me further if he hadn't already played baseball with my phone.

"Don't you love me, baby?" Percy whispered feverishly.

"Yes."

"Then tell me you love me."

"I love you," I said.

"Then *make* love to me."

"I'm just not ready." How many times did I have to tell him, I wondered.

Percy kept quiet. He just waited for a while, and then went for my panties again. Growing agitated, I pushed his hand away. Then Percy puffed heavily and turned his back to me.

I felt so bad. Rejected. Dejected. I really wanted to please Percy—just not in that way. So I reached over to hold him in my arms, trying to show him I cared, but he pushed my arm away with force and said, "Now you see how I feel."

Chapter 26

I didn't hear from Percy for a few days, and I didn't bother reaching out to him, either. Seemed like this was an ongoing pattern between us. He does something foul; I catch an attitude. Then he reels me back in with the bait of his romantic words. Fortunately, Jeselle and I were starting to get closer, so I didn't miss Percy as much this time around.

Percy ended up texting me on Wednesday, asking me to call him when I could. Since I already had a taste of his persistence, without delay I made sure the coast was clear, shut myself inside the bathroom, and called him, just to get it over with. The first thing he said was, "Hey, baby, I know it's hump day, but that doesn't mean we have to hump."

"Huh?" I asked, perplexed. I was sitting on the edge of the bathtub, trying to make this call quick and painless. I had no time for riddles.

"Hump day is considered Wednesday," Percy explained, "because it's the middle of the week. So I'm saying, even though it's Wednesday, I already got over the hump . . . get it?"

"Oh," I said, not amused. All joking aside, I still had some lingering problems with Percy and there was literally no rug in this bathroom to brush them under. I had to let him have it.

"Percy, I didn't appreciate the way you treated me at your father's house," I blurted. "Yelling at me . . . pressuring me for sex . . . I thought you said you loved me."

"I *do* love you," insisted Percy.

"But sometimes it doesn't feel like it."

"Listen, baby, I'm sorry, okay? I lost control."

"Yeah . . . tell me about it."

"Please don't be sarcastic with me," said Percy. I could tell he was monitoring the bass in his voice. Because real talk, if he started yelling at me again, I was ready to hang up on his crazy behind. And he knew it.

"Everybody loses control every once in a while," he explained. "And no disrespect, sweetheart, but you really need to start learning how to forgive people."

"But I have forgiven you," I snapped. "More than once!"

"Seems like you're not in the mood to talk," said Percy, sadly.

Between me and you, I wasn't in the mood. Percy had a way of twisting things around, always trying to make me feel like I was the one at fault. I missed him, yes, but I was getting tired of his mess. Percy was putting me through so much nonsense in such a short period of time. I wasn't sure what to think. If this was how relationships worked, maybe I needed to be single.

One thing was for sure though: I needed to get off this phone. *Now.*

Jeselle and I were about to take a walk around the neighborhood park. I was trying to show her simple pleasures, the same way Felicia had shown me.

"Anyway, I have to go now. Me and my homegirl are about to head out."

"Head out where?"

"The park," I said firmly, daring Percy to interrogate me.

He dramatically heaved a sigh and said, "Okay . . . once again, your friend comes first. . . . I already know the drill."

But Percy *didn't* know I had built up enough courage to show him how the dial tone feels. *Click.*

Percy called me right back.

At first, I wasn't about to answer. But I knew he was the type to keep on calling until I picked up the phone. So I answered the phone, eyes rolled to the ceiling.

"Yes?" I said with an attitude.

"Listen, Kate, let's not do this," Percy began, his voice mad humble now that he knew I meant business. "There was no need to hang up on me."

"Okay, sorry for hanging up, but I already told you I have to go."

"Can we please stop fighting?"

"I don't want to fight, either."

"Then can I see you again?"

"I don't know."

"Oh, so you *don't* want to see me?" Percy asked in a pitiful voice. "Are you determined to stay mad at me?"

"No . . . it's not that."

"Then what is it?"

"Well . . . if I see you again . . . it has to be outdoors."

"What? You don't trust me anymore?"

"I didn't say all that," I countered. "I'm just saying, why tempt ourselves? I'm not ready to have sex yet, and you can't seem to accept that. So it's better that we see each other outdoors."

Percy paused, and then spoke. "Okay . . . so if I promise not to try again, are you willing to come over? We can watch TV, or play cards, whatever you want to do . . . and I promise not to lay a hand on you."

"I don't think that would be a good idea."

"Okay," Percy said in a low voice. "I can respect that."

"Thanks for understanding."

"Anyway, I better let you get back to your little friend. Bye."

When I hung up the phone, my heart sank. I wasn't happy with the way things were going between us. I wasn't about to call Percy back, though. Maybe we needed some time apart. But to my surprise, two hours later, Percy texted me, asking me to call him.

I had just gotten back from my walk, and was feeling free and easy, but as I stood in the bathroom, staring at Percy's text, I felt like the walls were closing in on me.

I took a deep breath, and made the call.

"Hey, baby," Percy exclaimed. His voice sounded mad happy, like nothing had happened, like la-di-da!

"Hey," I said, in a lackluster voice.

"I just found out there's going to be a free concert at Boys and Girls tomorrow."

"Oh," I replied, still taken aback that he was calling me so soon.

"And guess who's performing."

"Who?"

"Fabolous!"

Now my ears perked up. I was feeling Fabolous. And his concert was free? Oh yeah, best believe I would be there. But really? A part of me wished I was going with my girls instead.

Chapter 27

The concert was set to begin at three o'clock, but I was out of the house before twelve. I was not trying to be late. No mistakes allowed. I wanted no reason for Percy to pop off on me, because, hey, you never know, I might just pop back.

I arrived in Bed-Stuy at 1:30 PM. Cobalt-blue sky. Sun beaming down on Brooklyn. It was a very beautiful day.

I was supposed to meet Percy in front of the Boys and Girls entrance at two thirty. So I had mad time to kill. First things first; I needed something to eat.

I headed to the pattie place located near the Utica Avenue train station. Once inside, I stared hungrily at the yellow cakes and bread pudding sitting behind thick glass. The line of people was dumb long. My stomach rumbled every two seconds; Jamaican music was blasting so no one could hear how hungry I was. As the line inched forward, I shifted from foot to foot, impatient as ever.

I was next in line to order, when I felt a tap on my shoulder. I swiveled around to face Charles, who was grinning from ear to ear. "Yo, shawty, you owe me a pattie," he said.

"Hey, Charles," I replied, smiling. "What brings you here?" I was so happy to see him, but playing it off, as usual.

"I spotted you as I was passing by. I swear, I could be anywhere in the world and I can always spot my girl, Kate."

"Okay, that's sweet. But fall back for a minute, please? I'm starving!" I turned to the lady behind the counter. "Miss, may I have one chicken pattie, please?"

"Aww, so well-mannered," joked Charles. "Too bad you're uncivilized when it comes to your homeboy. Tell me why you left a brother hanging on the Fourth?"

After paying for the pattie, I addressed Charles's remark, feeling guilty as ever. "My bad," I began, "things got really hectic that day."

"And my feelings got really hurt," Charles replied. "You had me stuck in the crib for no good reason."

"I'm really sorry. My bad." I looked down at the floor.

Charles patted my shoulder. "I'm only messing with you. I accept your apology. Nobody told me to wait inside the house, anyway. I had choices." Charles smiled and extended his fist for a pound. We pounded. We cool. Simple as that.

"Can you keep me company while I eat?" I asked, brightening up, as we walked out the store. It felt so good being next to Charles. I felt so relaxed, so *myself* with him.

"Where are we headed?" asked Charles.

"Fulton Park."

"So I'm guessing you're around the way for the Fabolous concert?"

"No doubt!"

"Meeting up with Felicia?"

"Nah," I said, not bothering to mention Percy. I was enjoying Charles too much right now. For some reason, I didn't even want to think about Percy.

Charles and I sat on a park bench under the shade and I dogged my pattie like a savage while Charles watched me. I didn't feel self-conscious at all. When I was done, Charles laughed at me and said, "You wolfed it, son!"

"Yeah, a sister was starving." I laughed.

Charles grabbed my paper bag, fished out a napkin, and caringly wiped the crumbs away from my mouth. "Thanks," I said, as my stomach took a quick dip into butterfly land. Oh man. Charles was starting to get to me again. My homeboy seemed to have a permanent spot in my heart.

"So you lookin' nice," said Charles, looking me up and down, at my plain old outfit.

"Thanks, you, too," I said, admiring his fresh white tee and criss-cross cornrows, wondering what broad fixed it for him, and growing resentful at the mere thought. I stared at his head for a minute before saying, "So you found one of your many girls to braid your hair, huh?" I didn't mean to sound jealous, but hey, I was.

"Not a girl," Charles corrected. "A grown woman from the African hair-braiding shop on Throop. How many times do I have to tell you there are *no* other girls right now? I'm still trying to get with *you*."

"Yeah, right." I smirked.

"Kate, I already told you I've slowed down a whole lot."

Slowed down. These words reminded me about our last conversation in front of the Garden. He had mentioned "slowing down" and "Naleejah" in the same sentence. I reminded him about needing to spill the gossip. "Still not a good time," he explained.

"Oh hell naw!" I protested, grabbing his arm. "You promised to tell me."

Charles suddenly grew very serious. He paused, and then spoke. "Well . . . how can I put this . . . Naleejah has a *House In Virginia*."

"She has a house?" I repeated in disbelief. "Wow, she must be tricking big-time! Who bought it for her?"

"Oh . . . I guess you never heard that term before."

"What term?" I asked, exasperated. "Quit with the riddles and tell me what's up."

Charles paused again, and then blurted, "Naleejah has HIV."

My bottom lip hit the floor. My hand flew to my mouth. As much as I couldn't stand the girl, my heart suddenly went out to her. "Oh my gosh. How'd you find out?" I asked in horror.

"Divine told me . . . he got a call from the clinic telling him he needs to get tested."

"Wow," was all I could say.

"I feel so messed up for my boy because he hit Naleejah *raw*."

"Oh my gosh." Tears started welling in my eyes.

"Yeah, and he didn't take the test yet. . . . He doesn't want to know."

"So, what if he unknowingly gives it to the next chick?"

"I know, right? See, that's why I *always* use condoms with girls like that," said Charles, shaking his head.

"Not just with girls like that . . . with everybody," I muttered. Charles needed to get his facts straight. "Nobody is immune to AIDS, no matter how innocent or fine. Everybody's status is suspect. Trust."

"I feel you," Charles replied. "But I'm careful. I got tested. I'm good."

"Well, I'm glad," I said.

"I still see Naleejah around the way," continued Charles. "She still looks the same. Same weight. Hair done. Wardrobe always on point. You can't even tell she has the virus . . . and that's the scary part."

I stared at the ground, still blinking back tears. Poor Naleejah with her low self-esteem, and neglectful parents . . . sleeping around to find love. The girl already had so many problems. And now she had a *deadly* one.

Charles lifted my chin and stared at me with concern. "Are you okay?"

I nodded, but I was lying.

"See, I told you this wasn't a good time to tell you."

"Yeah . . . I should've believed you."

A part of me wanted to reach out and call Naleejah. But her number was in last year's trash. And I didn't feel comfortable making a pop-up visit to her house. Face to face, what could I say to make things okay? All I could do was wish the best for her.

Charles, seeing I was really shaken, reached over and pulled me close to him. I put my head on his chest and rested for a while. I don't know how much time passed before he pulled me away and said, "Okay, now I need you to cheer up. Let's head to Boys and Girls. My homeboys will be there, but I'll tell them I'm chilling with you."

Oh, no. Percy.

I checked my watch. Twenty minutes to spare. I breathed a huge sigh of relief.

Charles was up on his feet, but I stayed put. "Why you sitting there like a statue? You rolling with me, or what?"

"Um, I have to wait for somebody," I said.

"Here?"

"Yeah," I lied. Even in his absence, Percy had me shook.

"Well, I'm not going to let you sit here by yourself."

"It's broad daylight," I said testily. "I'm good."

Shoo, Fly Boy, Shoo!

Charles paused and stared at me for a minute. Then he said, "All right yo, I'm out."

Finally.

I watched Charles walk toward Malcolm X Boulevard. Then I made my move. I looked both ways and ran across the street to stand at the entrance of Boys and Girls High. I was fifteen minutes early—just in case. Just to be safe.

But ten minutes later, my safety net was torn up from the floor up. Charles and a troupe of his boys came walking up the block, headed straight toward me. I wanted to sink inside the sidewalk.

I hoped with all my heart that Charles would just wave at me and keep it moving. But nope, he stopped dead in front of me, and kept his boys moving. "I'll get back up with y'all on the inside," he called after them.

Charles turned to me and said, "So we meet again." But before he could say anything else, a pretty cinnamon-brown girl rocking wavy *real* hair and a killer pink minidress rolled up on Charles from behind, showing all her teeth. "Hey, Charles," she said in a flirty voice.

"Hey, what's up, Rosa," said Charles, barely looking her way.

"Did you see Melanie go inside yet?"

"Naw, I just got here," he said, distractedly.

"So are y'all gonna be in the back, or the front?"

"Not sure yet," Charles replied with a shrug.

Rosa was acting thirsty, but Charles didn't seem interested in quenching. A spark of jealousy ran through me, but at the same time, I wanted Rosa to win her flirty game. Then maybe she could lure Charles away from my vicinity before Percy showed up.

The next thing I knew, Charles said, "Yo, Rosa, I'll catch you on the inside, okay? I'm talking to my shorty right now."

Rosa and I wore the same shocked face at Charles's words: "My shorty."

Really?

As flattered as I was, I wasn't grinning. My mind was totally fixed on Percy's reaction if he caught me standing with Charles. So the minute Rosa sashayed away, I got busy trying to think of a way to get rid of Charles. I was as nervous as ever and he sensed it. "What's wrong, Kate?"

"Still thinking about Naleejah," I quickly said. This was half true. I was really sad about my ex-homegirl, but more panicky about Percy.

"Try not to think about it," said Charles. Taking me off guard, he reached out and wrapped me up into a big bear hug.

Then *boom.*

As if some force of nature was playing a bad joke on me, tell me why Charles chose to embrace me the split second Percy rolled up in his car?

There was a parking spot two cars away from where we stood. In a snap, Percy whipped the Avenger into the spot, hopped out of the car, and slowly approached us. He didn't look happy at all.

Chapter 28

Percy's lips were set into a thin firm line. He didn't say a word.

"Hey, Percy," I stuttered.

He ignored my greeting, looked over at Charles, then looked at me and said, "Can I talk to you for a second?" Without waiting for a reply, Percy grabbed my hand and pulled me away from the front gate that I had been trembling up against.

"Kate, are you okay?" Charles asked, following after us.

"Yeah, yeah, I'm fine," I said, not wanting Charles to get involved. This was my battle. I got myself into it. Now I had to get myself out.

Charles lightly touched my arm. "Are you sure? Everything cool?"

"Yeah, yeah, it's cool," I insisted.

Percy put on a friendly mask and said, "My man, I just need to talk to my girl in private, a'ight?"

Charles ignored Percy and fixed me with a serious stare. "If you need me, holler at me, okay?"

"Oh stop, I'm good," I said, faking a laugh.

Charles finally walked away. I didn't dare look after him, fearing what Percy would say. The evil jealousy in his eyes was frightening.

We crossed Fulton Street, away from the concert. I was bewildered beyond words. Percy's hand squeezed my arm so hard, it felt like he was taking my blood pressure. He walked me down Stuyvesant

Avenue, stopped short at the corner, and then hemmed me up against a mailbox.

I was scared to death. Bad as I am, I can't beat a man.

"So you messing with that punk clown, aren't you?" demanded Percy. The vein in his forehead suddenly popped out.

"No, I'm not," I stuttered. "Charles is just a friend."

"You think I'm stupid, huh? I bet he's the one smashing it . . . that's why you won't give me any."

"No, he's not," I said, now close to crying. "Why are you yelling at me? I'm telling you the truth!"

Percy grabbed me by my top and said, "You're lying, Kate. I know you're lying. That's the same punk you were hugging up on like a slut at the Garden."

Whoa.

Two blows hit me at once. First, Percy had just fixed his mouth to call me a slut. Second, that he had been watching me the whole time I was with Charles at the Garden on the Fourth of July. Who does that? How creepy.

I stared at the vein in Percy's forehead, at the red splotches on his cheeks, and the crazy look in his eyes. Any love I had for Percy vanished at that moment. This was not the same man I had fallen in love with. This was a crazy man who I had to get away from. Fast.

I made a move to leave. Percy yanked me back like a rag doll. "Don't walk away from me when I'm talking to you."

"Get off me, please," I said, calmly.

"Where you think you're going?" he demanded. "I'm not finished talking to you!"

"But you're yelling at me . . . and you don't believe anything I say. What do you want from me?" I blubbered.

I swear, this whirlwind love affair was turning into a freaking nightmare.

Tears welled up in my eyes. Why? Why did I trust this man with my heart when he couldn't even trust *me*? I never flirted with anybody in front of him. In fact, *he* was the one flirting with the waitress, and who knows who else? I decided to hit him with this fact. I was so hurt, I had to fight back. "Percy, did I say anything to you when you disrespected me?"

"When did I disrespect you?" he demanded.

"Flirting with that waitress."

"Say what?" Percy boomed. "You lucky I didn't drop your little black behind to be with her!" he shouted. "She looks way better than you. I can be with anybody I want. But here I am wasting my time with a loser like you."

Wow. Really? What a low blow.

Something inside me flipped, like a courage switch. Percy's words were so hurtful, so dead wrong; I had no choice but to find my own voice. "So, if I'm such a loser, why are you stressing me then? Calling me off the hook, and begging me to be with you? If you can have anybody you want, then go be with them. Stop stressing me!"

"Please, B—, nobody is stressing you," said Percy with a dismissive wave. "Who are you to stress? Nobody wants you anyway."

"Then leave me alone!" I shouted.

Better yet, let me leave *him* alone, I thought. Why was I standing here taking all of this crap from Percy when I had two feet and my own mind to walk away? Percy had no right to detain me. Bump that. I had come all the way to Bed-Stuy to see a Fabolous concert, and a Fabolous concert I would see.

Reviving the courage that had almost died inside of me, I took one last look at Percy and mentally broke free. "I'm *out*," I said, tasting freedom on the tip of my tongue.

I spun on my heels and headed back to Boys and Girls. Held my head high with every step down the block. It felt so good to leave the crazy man right where he stood. But when I made it to the corner of Fulton Street, I looked to my right.

There was Percy.

In the flesh.

Leaning against the STOP sign across the street, his sinister stare aimed dead at me.

Chapter 29

I had to make a sudden change of plans. If I allowed Percy to follow me inside Boys and Girls High, I'd be feeding him to a vicious pack of lions. Man, listen: If Charles witnessed Percy disrespecting me, he would fly Percy's head, not to mention his boys carried weapons. Since jail time over me was out of the question, I had to steer clear of the school.

I hurried down Fulton Street, every few seconds glancing over my shoulder. Percy kept ten feet behind me, probably playing innocent in case I screamed for help. But I wasn't about to scream. I didn't want to bring any attention to myself. This was *my* battle that I had to fight. I got myself into this mess; I had to get myself out.

Finally. Utica Avenue train station.

I raced down the steps. Out of nowhere, Percy rushed up from behind, grabbed my upper arm, and spun me around. We stood on the middle of the staircase, mean-grilling each other.

"Why won't you talk to me?" he demanded.

I just stared at him like he was stupid, because he was.

"What do you expect me to say?"

"You know I love you," he suddenly cooed. "So why are you doing this to me?"

"Doing *what* to you?" I demanded, shaking with anger.

"Why can't you be honest with me? Tell me what's going on between—"

I yanked my arm away from him. He was obviously nuts. I had already told him once, Charles is just my friend. Enough was enough.

I dug in my pocket for my Metrocard, and made a move toward the turnstile. But Percy grabbed my arm again and said, "Why do you keep walking away from me?"

"Can you let go of my arm, please? I'm done talking to you."

"Oh, it's like that?"

"Yeah, it's like that," I said calmly. "I'm too ugly for you anyway . . . so go ask Bianca for her number."

"I already did," Percy spat.

"Then call her," I said.

"I will," he replied. "So, matter of fact . . . give me back my phone, slut."

"Wow, so I'm a slut now?"

"A sloppy black slut," said Percy, emphasizing every word. "I can't believe I even wasted my time with someone like you."

Wounded by Percy's words, but determined to hide it, I furiously dug up the BlackBerry from my pocket, tempted to throw it at him. Then again, nah, I had my dignity.

I planned to hand the phone back like a lady, but Percy snatched it savagely from me. "Now you can't call the punk you been cheating on me with."

"Nobody's cheating on you," I snapped. "So go ahead and take your little *tracking device* back. I don't care."

I was about to step away when Percy lifted his right arm, hauled back, and slapped the living mess out of me. I saw stars and lights flash before my eyes. My hand flew up to my cheek; it burned like hell. It felt like Percy's handprint was actually branded on my face. No one was around to ask, "Did that just happen?" I couldn't believe it.

"See what you made me do?" Percy yelled.

I pressed my hand against my cheek, staring at Percy in disbelief. He had the craziest look in his eyes. This was one of the scariest moments in my life. I had been through hell and back throughout my time in foster care, but I never had someone who claimed to love me, put their hands on me to hurt me. I was shaken to my core.

"See, if you didn't make me so mad that wouldn't have happened." Percy grabbed my arm again and held it like a vice grip. I was too afraid to move. "Why are you acting this way, huh? Don't you know how much I love you?"

Just then, an A train rumbled into the station. People started climbing up the stairs. Now that I had witnesses, I could finally leave Percy where he stood.

Adding to my confidence, I spotted a police officer walking toward us, like a savior fallen from heaven.

I twisted from Percy's grip and darted through the turnstile without looking back.

I sat in a quiet corner on the A train with my feet up on the seat, knees up under my chin. I held my head down so no one could see me crying. A woman tapped me on my shoulder and asked if I was okay, but I had no strength to look up to see who she was. At my stop, I dried my eyes with my T-shirt, but during my walk to Common Grounds, I was crying again.

I had to pull myself together before I stepped inside the group home. I didn't want anyone to know what had just happened to me. I was too embarrassed and ashamed. There was no one I could talk to but myself.

I can still feel Percy's handprint burning on my face. How could Percy do this to me? How could Percy tell me he loves me in one breath, and then hit me the next? I can no longer deny it; Percy is not the man for me. I need to put an end to this relationship, this abusive, unhappy relationship. My heart is finally telling me what my mind knew all along. Percy is just another piece of the sorry puzzle called My Life. All I ever want is love; all I ever get is hurt.

Chapter 30

It was five o'clock in the morning, and I couldn't go to sleep for nothing. The memory of the previous day's events pounded in my skull like an unbearable headache. Writing about Percy in my journal didn't help shed any logical light on him. My mind was split in two confused pieces. Half of me was completely done with the madman. The other half missed the gentleman. Percy was the first guy I ever loved. This was the first *real* relationship I ever had. It wasn't going to be as easy to erase Percy completely from my heart. But I knew no matter what, I had to let him go.

I tossed and twisted in my bed, feeling restless and crazy confused. The terrible things Percy said to me kept revolving around in my brain. How could Percy fix his mouth to call me a sloppy black slut? I thought I was his ebony doll.

Did Percy love me, or did he not? Had this all been a bad dream? My mind was such a murky mess right now. I desperately needed to talk to someone. But who?

I couldn't talk to my closest friends. I was too embarrassed to admit that I had gotten myself hit. I could already hear Felicia saying, "I told you so," and I could already picture Jeselle, clapping her hands and yelling, "Stomp Percy out!"

Tisha was the only person I could talk to. But she was about to leave on her honeymoon. I wasn't sure of the exact date, but she was headed to Paris soon enough, and didn't need to be hearing any drama from me.

Still, I desperately needed to talk to someone. I battled myself on whether to call Tisha or not, and finally lost the battle. I had to call her ASAP, or I was about to lose my freaking mind.

Tisha usually turned her phone off after hours, so I planned to leave a message on her cell phone, marked *urgent.* I quietly crept downstairs to make the call before the whole house woke up.

I anticipated voice mail. So imagine my dismay when Tisha answered her phone in a groggy voice.

"Oh, my gosh, I'm so sorry," I stuttered. "I didn't mean to wake you."

"Kate? What's wrong?" Tisha asked in a worried tone.

"Well . . . you told me to call you if I ever needed your advice. I really need it now."

"Why? What happened?" she asked, now sounding more alert.

I gave her a brief summary of my relationship with Percy, saving the slap for last.

I could almost hear Tisha's bottom lip hit the floor. "Please tell me you're okay."

"Yeah, I'm okay," I said. "And don't worry . . . I'm not planning to go back to him. I'm just feeling a little confused right now. I can't understand how things went so wrong, so fast."

"Well, just be glad Percy showed you his true colors so soon. Some guys can hide their craziness for years."

"True."

"Do you love him?"

"I don't know . . . well, no . . . not anymore."

"Did you sleep with him?"

"No . . . but I was going to."

"Just be glad you didn't. You saved yourself from a complete loser. I can't believe he laid his hands on you."

I didn't want Tisha to get the idea that Percy was a *complete* loser, so I told her about all the nice things he had done for me. But Tisha wasn't having that. "Kate, I'm sorry to tell you, but abusers do nice things to *keep* you, not because they *love* you."

"Oh . . . okay . . . well, it's just that . . . I guess a small part of me is just wondering if this was a one-time thing . . . him hitting me, I mean . . . nobody's perfect, and—"

Tisha cut me off before I could complete my sentence. "Listen, a pigeon-toed guy isn't perfect, a guy who talks with his mouth full isn't perfect, but a guy who disrespects you and puts his hands on you is damaged goods. Send Percy back, without looking back. It never gets better, Kate. It only gets worse."

I remained silent, taking in the power of her words.

Tisha continued. "Listen, as much as I love my husband, if Greg hit me today, I'd be signing divorce papers tomorrow. Trust me, I don't play that. Greg would be straight out of luck. Do you hear me?"

How could I *not* hear her? Tisha was yelling in my ear now. And when I made the mistake of saying, "Feels like I'm always out of luck . . . I'm the original bad luck girl," Tisha started yelling even louder.

"Kate, bad luck has nothing to do with what happened to you! You *chose* to walk into this relationship with your eyes closed. You bumped your damn head, and now I'm knocking some sense into it. Don't ever let a man make you feel like you're nothing, like he's doing you a favor by being with you. How many times do I have to tell you, you're worth more than that?"

I was sniffling over the phone now. This was all so hard, so embarrassing.

"I don't understand you, Kate. Last year, you let some girl make you feel like you weren't good enough to be with her, and this year you got some guy doing the same thing? This isn't about luck; this is about your poor choices . . . your obvious lack of self-esteem. Understand me?"

I had nothing to say.

Tisha continued. "How many times do I have to tell you that you had no choice with your parents, but you can choose more wisely when it comes to your friends and your men?"

"But I didn't *choose* Percy," I objected. "He chose me . . . and I didn't *expect* to fall in love with Percy. It just happened."

"Well, don't be *falling* in love then," snapped Tisha. "Watch where you're going next time, or you'll end up hurting yourself again. No more falling. You need to *walk* into a relationship with your eyes wide open. And when you see warning signs, you need to get out fast. Understand me?"

"Yes," I said, still sniffling. "I understand."

Tisha finally calmed down and said, "I don't mean to be yelling at you, but I'm just so shocked and upset."

She sounded *really* upset, and I didn't even mean to upset her, or keep her on the phone this long. I wanted to hang up now.

"See, I wish you would've called me before you got in this deep," Tisha continued. "You and I are long overdue for a lunch date, but I'm flying to Paris today for my belated honeymoon."

Paris *today*? Of all the days to call Tisha, I had to pick the day of her honeymoon? Worst timing in the world strikes again. Way to go, Kate.

"I'm so sorry for calling you this early," I said. "I had no idea you were leaving today."

"Listen, I'm glad you called me," said Tisha. "I have a lot going on, but I want to be there for you when I can. You understand me?"

"Thanks, Tisha."

Before getting off the phone, Tisha made me promise to have a final exit strategy with Percy. She told me it was dangerous to leave him without a plan. "Be respectful to him, but firm," she told me. "Don't give him any reason to hope he still has a chance to get back with you." Then Tisha gave me important Web sites to look at and phone numbers I could call:

www.loveisrespect.org—1-866-331-9474
National Domestic Violence Hotline—1-800-799-SAFE (7233)
www.breakthecycle.org

Apparently, I wasn't the first girl to be going through this, because Tisha had all of the info at her fingertips. I felt so protected and relieved when I got off the phone with her.

I was not alone.

There was no doubt about it now. Percy did not love me. Percy was dangerous. I had to set him completely free. It would be hard, but I had to be strong. I owed it to myself to stand up for myself, or else, fall back into Percy's dark and twisted little world.

Chapter 31

Hi, Kate," said a stranger's voice. A squeaky little girl's voice.

"Who's *this?*" I asked, perplexed. The only female who ever called me at the group home was Felicia—back when we were talking. This was surely not Felicia. This girl sounded like a ten-year-old. I looked at Makeba, who had handed me the phone. Confusion was written all over my face. Makeba shrugged and walked away.

"Hello, Kate?" Now it was Percy on the line.

My bottom lip hit the floor. Really? I couldn't believe his everlasting nerve. My chest tightened and heaved up and down like it does when I'm about to have a fight. How dare Percy have some unfamiliar chick calling my crib, let alone calling me *period*, after all the dirt he had done to me? Did he really think letting a few days pass would erase my freaking memory?

"Why are you calling me?" I demanded. "And why are you getting other people involved?"

"Oh, that was just my little cousin Shante . . . I didn't want to get you in trouble."

"Oh, how nice of you," I said, rolling my eyes to the ceiling.

"Listen, baby, I'm sorry about what happened between us, okay? Let's just put it behind us. I'm really sorry."

"No you're not," I snapped. I was about to go off on him, but Venus was nearby, watching TV in the living room. I didn't want her in my business. I wanted to brush my big mistake safely under the dirty carpet.

Lowering my voice, I said, "Listen, please don't call here anymore, okay?"

"Can't we talk about this in person?"

"No, we can't."

"Why not?"

"Well, this sloppy black slut is incredibly busy right now."

"Sweetheart, you know I didn't mean that, right? I was just having a bad day. Don't you know how much I love you, Kate? Can we please try to work things out?"

"There's nothing to work out," I said. "You'll never change."

"But I need you in my life, Kate. . . . Please don't do this to me."

"Do *what* to you?" I snapped. "You're the one who did it to *me*. Don't try to turn things around like you always do."

It felt so good talking back to Percy with full force. But I was about to go against Tisha's advice and completely lose my temper with him. So this back-and-forth mess had to be cut short. Luckily, the excuse of my group home's fifteen-minute rule saved my day. But it didn't save my week. I got a call from the same strange little girl every single day, and each time I had to play it off like I knew her, talk to Percy, and try my best not to cause a scene.

My cover-up routine was so exhausting. But Percy wouldn't take no for an answer. He needed to speak with me in person, he explained. He *had* to speak to me in person. "One last time."

But I knew Percy was only trying to reel me back into his tangled, drama-filled web in order to feed me more promises he would never keep. Nothing Percy could say would bait me back. I deserved so much better than Percy; and he did not deserve me. Like waking up from a deep sleep, I had finally come to my senses once and for all.

"Baby, just give me one more chance," Percy pleaded.

"Percy, it's over," I firmly said, hopefully for the last time. "Seriously, don't call here again."

Click.

Chapter 32

Bright and early in the afternoon, Ciara called for me from downstairs. "You have a visitor," she announced.

Oh really? I thought. Was it Felicia again? It was going to be so uncomfortable facing her right now. Trust me, I was planning to call her, but not just yet. I was still too embarrassed. Too ashamed.

I climbed down the stairs with my heart stuck in my throat.

The front door was cracked halfway open. Apprehensively, I inched up to the threshold to find not Felicia, but a preteen in a ponytail staring at me with big hazel eyes.

"Hi, I'm Shante."

My bottom lip hit the floor.

"Percy wants to see you," she said. "He's waiting for you across the street."

Wow. This was some bull.

Percy's blind ambition was inescapable. This guy was absolutely nuts. Not nutty over me, just plain old nuts. I was far from flattered by his persistence. Percy's persistence had nothing to do with love. Percy didn't love me. I had to keep reminding myself of this simple fact, told myself to never, never look back. The good times we shared had been a fairy tale. Our relationship was over. The End. And apparently, I needed to tell this to Percy's face because he wasn't getting it. Bad idea, but what else could I do? Him showing up at my house, and bringing little girls into the situation was not a good look. The madness could not go on. I had to set Percy straight one last time.

I didn't want Shante to witness this. She was too young to be caught up in this dramatic mix. "Wait right here," I told her. Then I went back inside the house and got Ciara. I pretended that I needed to "get busy with my man real quick" and asked her to sneak Shante past Belinda's snoring face, straight to the back porch.

"Girl, go get your freak on!" said Ciara, wearing a mischievous smile. I wished I had a reason to smile back.

I took a deep breath, and bravely stepped outside into the warm afternoon air. Percy's Avenger was haphazardly parked in front of a fire hydrant, diagonally across the street from the group home. He was sitting inside the car, apparently waiting for me to hop inside. But please, homeboy, I'm not that stupid. I was planning to stand outside in full view.

Unfortunately, just as my awful timing would have it, I spotted Jeselle and Makeba coming up the block with grocery bags in their hands. So I quickly swung open the car door and ducked inside before they saw me. I didn't want them to have a clue about what was going on. Things could possibly get ugly.

As soon as I settled in my seat, Percy reached over to give me a hug. I flinched and ducked his arm. I didn't want him ever touching me again.

"Is something wrong, sweetheart?"

Come on now. What kind of dumb as dirt question was that? Seriously, I wondered if this dude had amnesia, or something. His forgetfulness was so convincing, I almost thought *I* was the one losing my mind.

"I got something for you." Percy reached into the backseat and handed me a lovely bouquet of red roses. Lovely as they were, I didn't take them. I just looked at the flowers as blooming lies. "These are for you, sweetheart," he explained, as if I was clueless.

"No, that's okay," I said, staring him dead in the face.

"Look, I'm really sorry for what happened," said Percy, putting the roses down. He stared at me for a long time. But the intensity in Percy's light brown eyes was no longer thrilling . . . quite chilling if you ask me.

"Percy, I accept your apology, okay?" I said, looking away from him. "But I can't get back with you. I'm sorry. I just can't."

"I don't understand," he began. "Why can't we try again? Every relationship has its problems."

"Not problems like *this*. You put your hands on me. And I'm sorry . . . but I'm not putting up with that."

"But why can't you forgive me?" asked Percy, sounding about ready to cry.

"I just told you. . . . You put your hands on me." I wore a determined look on my face.

"But I didn't mean to," whined Percy. "And I promise it won't ever happen again. . . . Please, baby, don't hold this against me. I need you in my life."

I already knew where this was headed; I was wasting my time and words on Percy. "Listen, I have to go." I reached for the door.

Without warning, Percy slapped my hand away from the handle.

"So you're really trying to leave me, huh?" he demanded, bass suddenly in his voice.

I was taken aback by Percy's sudden mood flip, but then again, why was I surprised? This was exactly why I needed to leave him. Dr. Jekyll could no longer hide.

"Look . . . I just need to be by myself right now," I said in a softer voice, trying to pacify this beast.

Percy quickly calmed down. His voice spun right back to sorry-mode, like magic. "Baby, I can't afford to lose you. Are you really going to leave me over a silly mistake I made? I didn't *mean* to slap you, okay? It was just a mistake."

"A mistake?" I repeated in disbelief, my anger rising again. "Stepping on my foot would be a mistake. *Slapping* me was deliberate as hell!"

"And you're going to hold that over my head, huh? Didn't I just say I was sorry?"

"Yes, and I accepted your apology. But I just can't be with you anymore. It's over."

Suddenly Percy's face darkened.

"So you want to be with that punk, don't you?" he shouted. "That's what this is all about, isn't it? Don't lie to me, that's what this is about, isn't it?"

I couldn't take it anymore. I made a move for the door. He slapped my hand away.

"So you're saying you don't want to be with me anymore?"

I had to get out of his car. Fast. I tried to open the door again, growing very, very afraid. A single blow has been known to kill, and Percy looked like he was ready to kill me. But every time I tried the door, Percy slapped my hand away.

"Please let me go," I said, my voice quivering.

Percy started pounding the steering wheel with clenched fists as he shouted, "You promised to never leave me. Now look at you. Running to the next man."

Since his hands were currently occupied beating up his steering wheel, I took this opportunity to make my escape. I shoved open the door, jumped out the car, and was about to run across the street. But Percy caught me by the arm in the middle of the road.

Fear and adrenaline pumped through me. I was about to make a run for it again, but Percy held my arm with a vise-like grip and snatched me up into a powerful bear hug.

"Get back in the car!"

"Get off me," I yelled. "It's over. Why can't you accept that?"

Percy fixed me with a look I'll never forget. "Get back in the car," he said between gritted teeth.

"No!"

We struggled for a few painful seconds, him wrenching my arm this way and that, hurting me, scaring me.

"Get off of me!" I shouted.

"Get in the car."

"No!"

"Okay," Percy began calmly, "if that's how you want it . . . if I can't have you, nobody can."

Before I could figure out what Percy meant by these words, he dragged me to the sidewalk, shoved me up against a gate, drew back his fist, and punched me dead in my stomach. I swallowed a mouthful of air, and doubled over in pain. Nobody had ever hit me so hard in my life. A scream caught in my throat. Before I could recover from the blow, Percy hit me again, and again, and again. . . . I tried to shield myself. But he grabbed my arms and pushed them away from my face, then began to pummel me like a punching bag.

I suddenly found my voice. I started screaming at the top of my lungs. "Stop!" I cried, "Please stop!" I hoped the neighbors would hear me. Somebody. Anybody. But Gravesend was a ghost town. Not a soul around. I soon realized I had to help myself.

My whimpering turned into a battle cry.

A black blur of rage came over me. I summoned all the strength I had and tried to fight him back. With every ounce of me, I tried to fight through the pain, block his blows. But I was no match for Percy. I threw punches and missed, so weak from the beating I was taking. Percy knocked me in my eyes, my mouth. It felt like he cracked one of my front teeth. He grabbed me by my shoulders and tripped me to the ground. Then all I saw was the white of his sneaker kicking the mess out of me. I covered my face, crying hysterically. "Please stop! Please—" My throat was hoarse from screaming.

The next thing I knew, I heard Jesselle's voice hollering, "Get off her!" and then I heard Makeba yelling, "Call the cops! Call the cops!" As their voices came closer, Percy pounded on me even harder. He banged my head against the sidewalk.

Then everything went black.

Chapter 33

I woke up in a hospital bed, shivering under a flimsy light-blue gown. I looked around the stark white room, confused and disoriented. Then it all came back to me. The beating, the shouts, the madness. How long have I been here? I wondered. My whole body throbbed in pain. An IV was hooked up to my arm. Gauze and tape covered my mouth. I couldn't talk; I could barely move. I lay stock-still like a frozen slab of meat.

The nearby window let in morning sunshine. But all I wanted to do was sleep. When I finally gathered the strength to hobble to the bathroom, I looked into the mirror and stared in disbelief at my black eye, my swollen face. I looked a hot mess, like a train wreck. Then again, a train wreck would've made much more sense. I couldn't believe that the man I once loved had done all this damage to me. This was my first time in the hospital since birth; and someone who claimed to love me had put me here. As bad as I looked, there was no way I wanted anybody I knew to see me like this.

So imagine my dismay when in walks Mrs. Cooper, the very next day; she had all six girls in tow, carrying a gang of "Get Well" helium balloons. I was half embarrassed, half touched because these girls had actually come to see me. Mrs. Cooper was the first to speak. "How are you feeling, honey? Are you okay?"

I nodded my head lightly because it hurt like hell. I reached over and grabbed the pen and pad a nurse had supplied me with earlier. "I'm okay," I wrote. There was no need to stir up pity going into detail about the excruciating pain I was in.

"We can't stay long, honey," said Mrs. Cooper. "All of us aren't supposed to be up here at one time."

Jeselle stepped forward. "Please, Mrs. Cooper, they mad lax up in this hospital. They ain't even make us sign in." Jeselle plopped down on my bed. "Shoot, I'm staying with my girl for as long as I want."

If I could have moved my mouth, I would've smiled at Jeselle. If I could have moved my body without so much pain, I would've hugged her, too. I wrote, "Thanks for coming," and held it up for all to see. Everybody was quiet. Just staring at me with pity in their eyes.

Jesselle broke the ice by saying, "Well, at least the bastard is in jail where he belongs. I hope *he* catch hella beat downs while he's there."

Percy, in jail?

The words "jail" and "hospital" just didn't go with the word "love." It was so hard to believe that our relationship had started out so beautifully only to end up like this.

But then again, I was still alive, so I made it out easy compared to some. The day before the attack, I had decided to do some research on abusive relationships. I read crazy stories. Scary stories. I learned some girls have to leave their relationships in a body bag. I left that library stunned out of my mind.

I almost lost my life for love.

I was so hurt and confused by this whole sad turn of events. But the Common Grounds crew really cheered me up. I looked at my balloons, and felt so cared about, so special. As much as we misunderstood and couldn't stand each other, the group home girls were my family. When I got back, I vowed to get along with each and every one of them even better, even if I had to try that much harder.

"All right ladies, Kate needs her rest," said Mrs. Cooper, though she looked like she needed it more. Her eyes were red, but I couldn't tell if she was tired or about to cry for me.

"Hold it down, Kate!" shouted out Jeselle.

The rest of the girls smiled and waved good-bye.

After everybody left, my thoughts turned to Felicia. I wasn't planning to tell her what happened until much later. If I told her now, she'd be hassling me about getting restraining orders.

I wasn't ready for aftermath arrangements. For now, Percy was in jail and that was more than enough to comfort me . . . for now.

Later in the day, I lay in bed with my eyes closed. Then I heard voices. "I think she's sleeping," someone whispered. I opened my eyes and that someone turned out to be Felicia, standing over me with Marlon and Charles by her side. Their presence was completely horrifying.

See, my group homegirls I had quickly gotten over; we'd all seen our share of traumatic times in the system. Felicia? Well, I could even handle her company; after all, she's my best friend, the one person in the world who knows almost everything about me. But Charles and Marlon? Oh man, I was mortified. Members of the opposite sex, witnessing what one of their own had done to me. I felt sick to the pit of my stomach, as they inched up closer to my bed. I wanted to pull the covers over my head and play dead.

"Hey, Kate," the boys said in unison.

The genuine look of concern fixed on both of their faces instantly stopped me from tripping. I quickly came to my senses, realizing that Charles and Marlon had nothing to do with Percy's horrible actions. They were visiting me because they cared. They were good guys. Percy could never compare.

"Hey, girl," said Felicia, in the saddest voice I ever heard.

Felicia was holding a giant card, Marlon a bouquet of sunflowers, and Charles an adorable pink and white "Get Well" teddy bear.

I slowly sat up. A streak of incredible pain shot through my back like a bullet. I struggled to reach for my pad. Charles could tell I was struggling, so he handed it to me.

"Thank you for coming," I wrote.

All three of my friends looked at me with so much sympathy in their eyes. I tried to ignore their compassionate stares. Awkward silence filled the room. Felicia was the first to speak up. "Well, Kate, you can't deny our connection now. Something told me to call the group home to check up on you . . . and Jeselle told me everything." Charles sat down at the foot of my bed, removed his iPod earbuds, and said, "I'm so sorry this happened to you." He shook his head. "Percy is such a sorry excuse for a man."

"For real," added Marlon. "A sorry excuse."

"You deserve so much better, Kate," said Felicia.

Charles continued his train of thought. "The day I saw you with him, I *felt* something was wrong, but you played it off so well, I tried to be chill. I wish I would've stepped to him then. Trust me, though, I got mad peoples on the inside, from Rikers to San Quentin. Fly one kite and Percy is a dead man. Believe that."

I wrote, "Please, don't. He's not worth it."

"Man, listen, I'm so sorry this happened to you," said Charles, shaking his head. "I don't know what to do."

The mood in the room was getting too melodramatic. So I drew a smiley face and pointed to it. Charles forced a chuckle and touched my leg over the sheet. "You better keep your head up, you hear me?"

"Her birthday is coming up, too . . . sweet sixteen," said Felicia, trying to force a cheerful topic in the mix.

"Yeah, I remember," said Charles. "My girl is getting old."

"We all need to do something together," said Marlon.

"No doubt, I'm down," Charles replied.

Wow, I thought, Charles was so cool. Felicia and Marlon are far from his type of hangout partners, but he was still willing to hang with them—unlike Percy, the loner, who had no friends of his own and had tried to isolate me from everybody. What was I thinking getting involved with a guy like Percy? Well, I *wasn't* thinking, that was the problem. Never repeating this mess again, that was my solution.

I had too much to live for to be getting sucked into another abusive relationship. Surviving Percy was like falling off a cliff and living to tell about it. Wished I didn't have to learn the hard way, all bandaged up and in so much aching pain; but at least I had learned. Relationships are hard, but they're not supposed to hurt. I can't even picture another guy trying to control me, push me around, talk down to me. Please, I'll kick his behind to the curb and ask questions later. Felicia and Tisha were right: I deserved so much better than Percy.

And at least I now understood what a good relationship looks like: Felicia and Marlon, Ted and Lynn. No disrespect and drama in their world, just petty little arguments every now and then. So if I couldn't have the real thing, I'd rather be alone.

"I can't wait for your stitches to come out," said Charles. "I want to see that pretty smile of yours."

Charles got up and walked toward the head of my bed. He clicked on his iPod, gently placed one earbud in my ear, and the other one in his. "So Beautiful" by Musiq Soulchild was playing. Charles was looking at me with so much concern in his sparkling dark brown eyes. In an instant, a magical atmosphere flowed throughout my hospital room. Felicia and Marlon seemed to disappear.

"Want you to know . . . so beautiful," Charles sang.

"My favorite song," I wrote.

"See, you and Felicia aren't the only ones with a connection." Charles winked at me.

Charles seemed so different these days, like a changed man. So much more chill and mature. Not so thirsty for booty like before. Shucks, the old Charles would've been bumping "Birthday Sex" in my ear.

A short, burly nurse came into the room, and told my friends visiting hours were over. I needed my bandages changed.

"Get well soon, so we can hang out," said Charles. He kissed my forehead.

Felicia kissed me on the cheek. "Stay strong, we've got things to do!"

"I say we go bowling," said Marlon.

"I never bowled in my life," piped in Charles, "but I'm down!"

"Thanks for stopping by," I wrote. "I can't wait to hang with y'all."

But when I got out of the hospital, I didn't hang with anybody right away. I needed some time to myself, time to figure out why I kept getting involved with the wrong people. I had to ask myself this question, and actually answer it this time, before I repeated the same mistake.

Obviously my self-esteem wasn't where it should have been; so I needed to raise it higher, out of reach from haters and abusers. I needed to be around people who made me feel good about myself, namely people like Felicia, my eternal homegirl, who always believed in me and never put me down.

But even Felicia had a life outside of me, traveling with her parents, hanging with the Stuck-up-Duo, and of course, there was Marlon.

I had to get my own life, too.

So when school started, the first thing I did was sign up to be a math tutor; I rocked math equations like it was nothing, so might as well get in where I fit in. Then I made an appointment with Children's Services to see about becoming a mentor for a younger girl in foster care. Tisha used to continuously remind me, "There's always someone out there who has it worse than you." So why shouldn't I help another young girl make it through?

I had already helped my girls at Common Grounds. After seeing me laid up in the hospital, every single one of them vowed to keep their eyes wide open when it comes to boys and abuse. We even made a pact to reach out to each other if any one of us got trapped in an abusive relationship. "There's nothing to be ashamed of," I had told them.

Reaching out is the right thing to do. But staying quiet and hiding behind dark glasses is dead wrong, and not the way to cope with the pain. In fact, days after I had gotten out of the hospital, I still looked like a one-eyed raccoon, with a black half-moon underneath my right eye taking forever to heal. I didn't try to hide it. No sunglasses on my face.

One day, I overheard Ciara explaining my black eye to a homegirl that she had snuck into the home. The girl had stared at me longer than necessary when we were introduced. Guessed she was curious; I couldn't blame her.

I was about to come out onto the back porch where they sat, when I heard the girl say, "Oh hell no! That could never be me. Let some guy try to put his hands on me. She's stupid."

Stupid? Excuse me?

Part of me was pissed that Ciara was actually spreading my personal business; the other part was determined to set the record straight. And this was the part that had me boldly stepping outside the door with a mouthful to say. "Oh, yes, it could be you," I blurted, while pointing to my eye with no shame. "Nobody is immune from abuse. Tough girls, smart girls, pretty girls, rich girls, white girls, black girls . . . even grown women get abused. Depending on where your self-esteem is on any given day, *anybody* can fall prey. So please don't get it twisted, okay?"

The girl's eyes were big with shock, maybe from my words, or maybe because I had busted through the door out of nowhere. Whatever the case, I really hoped she understood. You never know how you'll deal with a situation until you're actually in the situation. Never thought this could happen to me. Now I knew.

When it was time to leave Common Grounds, I was actually sad to go. Dirty house and all, I had mad love for all the girls I was leaving behind. We had more bad times than good in a short period of time, but these girls had my back during my darkest hour, and I would never forget them for that. Jeselle cried the hardest when my bags were officially packed.

"Girl, you act like I'm headed to Siberia," I joked, trying to keep the mood light. "The Bronx isn't that far."

"Shut up, silly," Jeselle said, between sniffles. She hugged me so long and so tight, like she wanted to come with me. I wished I could take her, but she wasn't ready for Green Hills. Their rules were off the hook. Strict curfew, maintaining grades, actual chores—what? Jeselle would be ready to choke a chick if she had to live there.

Green Hills was everything Mrs. Cooper had promised, to my relief. Big clean home in a beautiful section of the Bronx. Nice and friendly staff, and crazy cool girls who were on the same page as me, all about their school grind. It was going to take some time for me to get used to their routine, but I was looking forward to knowing them, to growing with them. This year was all about growing and learning, and never looking back.

I'm a survivor. Always have been. Always will be.

Chapter 34

It wasn't until the middle of September that I felt ready to return to familiar faces. It started out with a phone call from Felicia on a sun-drenched Saturday afternoon.

"Hey, Kate!" Felicia exclaimed.

"Hey, girl, what's up?"

"Marlon and I bumped into Charles on the A train yesterday. He begged me to tell you to call him. I told him that I was busy begging you to call me, too. I mean . . . we don't hang out anymore. I miss you."

I chuckled at the animation in her voice. "Well, my homework is done, chores are straight. Are you free today?"

"Totally free, but . . . Marlon is with me. . . . Is that okay?"

"Um . . . well, I—"

Before I could cop a plea, Felicia thought to say, "Why not call Charles right now? I could get him on the three-way. Maybe he can come!"

"A'ight," I said, trying to hide the excitement in my voice. I missed my homeboy, too. I hoped Mr. Fly Boy was available.

Charles answered on the first ring. Surprisingly, he was ready to drop everything and come hang with us. Felicia assured him that she'd find something for us to do on the quick tip; Google was her best friend—after me.

Sure enough, twenty minutes later, Felicia called Charles and me back via three-way, her voice mad amped like a speaker. "OMG! Jazmine Sullivan is performing at Central Park. We have to go, you guys!"

"That's what's up," I exclaimed. "What time do we have to be there? A sister is way up in the Bronx."

"Show starts at three," said Felicia. "But we should be there by at least two o'clock so we can get a good spot."

Felicia laid out the logistics like a perfect event planner. And thanks to her, we all managed to meet up at Central Park, on time, with no problems.

The day was hot and beautiful. And so was Charles. First, I was surprised to see he had cut off all his hair. His short waves were back, smooth and precise. He wore a blue and white jersey top with baggy khakis hanging off his behind just right, and he rocked super clean white K-Swiss sneakers. His dark-brown chocolate skin glistened in the sunshine.

Wow, he looked mad good, felt mad good, smelled mad good when I hugged him hello. No words were exchanged. We just stared at each other like mad. Our chemistry was crazy intense.

To deflect my feelings, I jokingly asked, "Why'd you cut off your lovely locks?"

Charles smirked. "Shoot, if I waited for *you* to braid my hair, I would've gone bald from old age!"

Suddenly feeling awful and completely embarrassed, I looked down at the ground and said, "I'm really sorry for that. My bad."

Charles touched my shoulder. "Why are you tripping, Kate? You know I'm only joking."

Flashbacks of Percy.

After all the guilt games Percy had played on me, it was hard to take a joke. But instead of explaining myself, I quickly pulled myself together, and turned my attention to my other homies. Felicia and Marlon were keeping it simple in plain white tees and baggy shorts. "Good to see y'all," I exclaimed, giving them both big hugs.

We hopped on the long, snaking line that slithered forward at a slow pace. "Man, when they gonna let a brother in?" asked Charles.

As we waited and waited, the sunbeams were starting to get to me. I looked up at the sky and said, "I really don't need to be in this sun . . . black as I am." Then I laughed at my own joke—by myself. No one else found my comment funny.

Charles cocked his head to the side and said, "I don't know what you're talking about . . . the blacker the Kate, the *sweeter* to me."

I playfully hit Charles and said, "You so silly."

But really? He was so sweet, trying to uplift me, upgrade me.

Evidently, Percy was not completely out of my system. My black eye was gone, my ribs were healed, but it would take much more time for me to fully recover from Percy's mental abuse.

Finally, the line started moving into the arena. In single file, my group trooped into a row of seats five levels high. Not bad. Kinda cool. We had a clear view of the stage. When Charles plopped down next to me, our legs touched. Electricity shot through my body like lightning. I wondered if he felt it, too.

"This is so exciting," said Felicia, sitting on the other side of me.

"I know, right!" I replied.

We had to sit through a few cool acts before Jazmine finally busted onto the stage, reppin' hard in her fabulous royal-blue outfit, glossy hair flowing in the wind. She got the crowd hype, and then started hitting them jazzy notes, rocking us from side to side. When she sung my favorite song, "I Need You Bad," Charles bent down to my ear and sung with her. "If I had you back in my land, I would prove that I could be a better man."

"Those are not the words!" I said, laughing.

"Those are *my* words I'm singing to you," Charles replied.

I smiled at him and shook my head in awe. He was so dang irresistible.

Charles peered over at Felicia and Marlon who were now leaning up against each other, holding hands. So Charles reached for my hand. But I pulled it away. Our intensity . . . it was too much for me to handle right now. I wanted Charles as bad as I needed the air I breathed, and I could feel deep in my heart that he wanted me, too; but still, I needed time. I'm not on that: on to the next one, hopping from boy to boy.

I needed to be alone for a while.

So when Felicia tried to sell me Charles as we stood on a long bathroom line after the concert was over, I had to tell her, "Fall back, Ms. Matchmaker!"

"But Charles is so in love with you!" she insisted.

"Well, if he is, then he's not going anywhere," I replied.

"Seems like he's really changing for the better, too," Felicia added. "I don't see him around the way with every girl in the world anymore."

"Time will tell," I said. "So give a sister some time, will ya?" I playfully tapped Felicia's arm.

"Okay, but don't wait too long. I'm just saying, somebody will snatch that fine boy up quick!"

I suddenly thought about Tisha and Greg, their love story twenty years in the making. "Nah, Felicia, as corny as it sounds . . . if it's meant to be, it will be."

"Okay, whatever you say," she replied with a shrug.

We joined Marlon and Charles, who were leaning up against the front gate, talking like old friends.

"So what's next?" asked Marlon, staring at Felicia with his usual lovey-dovey look.

No one had any suggestions, so I piped in. "Suddenly, I'm in the mood for hot chocolate." Maybe because Charles was so dang hot and chocolate.

"Odd choice, but I'm down," replied Charles with a chuckle. "So let's go get you some hot chocolate."

"I could use a Mocha Frappe," said Marlon, grabbing Felicia by the hand.

"Me, too," said Felicia. They walked way ahead of us down a rocky pathway. Charles slowed down to a stroll. Then he tried to hold my hand again. I let him this time.

Out of the blue, he looked over at me and said, "I just want you to know, I love being around you, Kate."

"I love being around you, too," I said, "but you already know what I've *just* been through. So please . . ."

My voice trailed off. I didn't want to start crying out of nowhere.

"Listen, Kate, I understand all of that. But please don't let Percy cheat you out of a relationship with me. We'd be so good together."

I slowly looked up at Charles. I didn't want to bring up the way he had hurt me in the past, but then again, I had to keep it real with myself and real with him, too. "Well, you weren't exactly faithful to me the first time around. Remember? Because it seems like you keep forgetting."

Charles paused and then spoke. "Okay . . . I'm not going to lie, most people *don't* change. But a few people do, and I'm one of the few. I don't run loose anymore, collecting girls' numbers for no reason—" He broke off his litany, whipped out his cell phone, and showed me his address book. A bunch of male names popped up as he scrolled through the list.

"See?" he said, staring at me, his eyes so serious. "Females get deleted quick these days. I don't have time for their games anymore. It's getting real old."

"Aw, that's probably just your *business* phone," I joked, keeping my defenses up.

Charles looked at me for a long minute. Then he put two fingers in his mouth and whistled to get Felicia and Marlon's attention. "Hey y'all, go ahead of us," he shouted. "We'll link back up at the entrance of the park."

"Not a problem," Felicia called back, grinning from ear to ear, clearly thinking something juicy was about to go down. Well, she was thinking dead wrong. No matter what Charles said to me, I was not about to rush into anything with him. I would stay in touch with him, watch his behavior over time, and then I'd make an informed decision based on what I saw. In other words, I would be walking into this relationship with my eyes wide open. No more bumping my head; it hurts too much.

We were standing under a tall oak tree when Charles gave my hand a gentle squeeze, and said, "Well, I hope you give me a chance someday."

A half smile touched my lips. I liked the sound of someday.

"So does that smile mean I have a chance?" asked Charles, flashing his boyish grin.

"A very good chance," I said, grinning back.

Charles, emboldened by my words, cupped my face in his warm hands, and said, "So how can I make our chances *great*?"

"By you being you, and letting me be me."

"Oh, I can definitely do that," said Charles.

I pursed my lips into a playful air kiss. Charles pretended to catch it. Then I removed his hands from my face and said, "Now that we're straight on the subject, let's go get our hot chocolate on!"

"No doubt." Charles smiled, grabbed my hand, and held it gently as we walked through the park. I snuck a glance at him and imagined his face as it would be in ten years, twenty years, thirty years. . . . I couldn't wait to grow with him, flow with him. Deep down in my heart, I knew that Charles was The One for me. The way he looked at me with so much love in his eyes could not be mistaken for anything but a strong and true connection between us. Our *someday* would most definitely come soon, but for now I had to focus on me.